FALL into MIDNIGHT

WILSON, NC

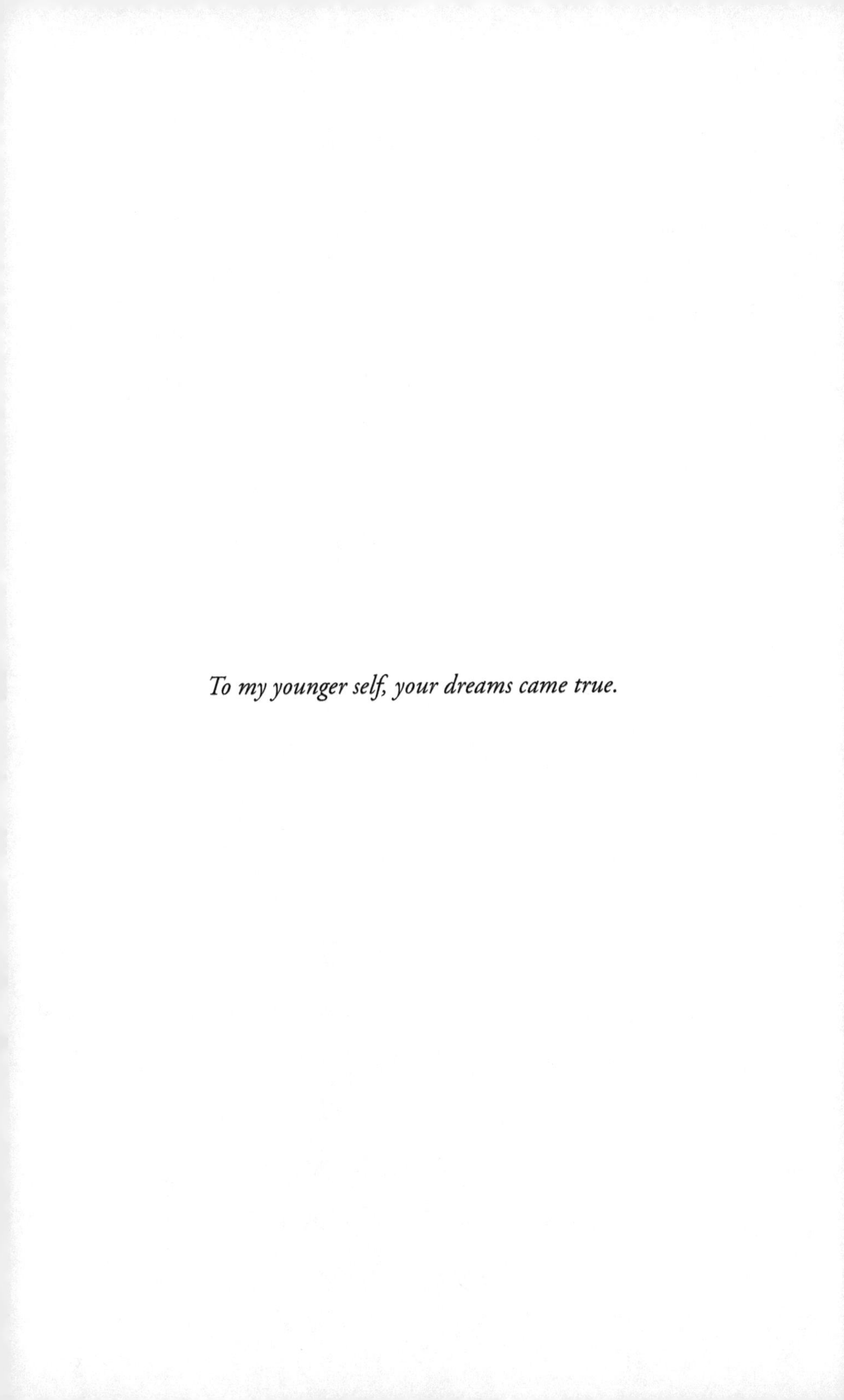

To my younger self, your dreams came true.

Scan the QR code with your phone to enjoy the
Spotify playlist that the author, Arden Coutts,
used as inspiration for *Fall into Midnight*.

Fall Into Midnight Spotify Playlist

The music starts, the lights dim, and reality fades.
Welcome to Club Midnight …

CHAPTER 1

Gray

The doors open, and an immediate rush of adrenaline spikes through my body as I watch clubgoers spill into Club Midnight and spread throughout the space. Women in barely-there dresses and men in everything from polo shirts to suits—as long as it has a collar, you can wear it in. All they want here and now at Midnight is to drink, dance, and maybe find someone to fuck.

It isn't the way she's dressed that catches my eye. Don't get me wrong, she looks stunning in the navy-blue jumpsuit she's wearing, but it's the way she moves in it that catches my eye.

She cuts through the crowd as if she's water running around rocks. Smoothly weaving her way between the manically gyrating bodies that seem possessed by the music filling every inch of the club. She is completely unfazed, yet her eyes are aware of every movement.

I can't help but watch her as she makes her way from the club's front door, through the dancefloor, to the bar at the back. I've never seen her here before. She's new, and I am intrigued. She's accompanied by a tall, dark-haired woman in a tight dress and a man and a woman dressed casually in jeans and collared shirts. It's easy to recognize the two as security, even though they're trying to seem casual. Yet how they carry themselves and constantly scan the space gives them away to the trained eye.

So, who is she, and why does she have protection in a nightclub?

I momentarily watch her group at the bar before shifting my gaze to the club door. Then my gaze sweeps from the dancefloor to the entrance, to the bar, and back again. Pausing to check the club's darker corners to ensure everything is clear. It's Saturday night, and without fail, there will be fights. It's a little past midnight, and we've already broken up multiple altercations.

I adjust my suit jacket and earpiece to scan the crowd for troublemakers. I have a good vantage point from my post on the back staircase. If you don't count the pockets of pitch darkness that make up some of the more sinister corners, I can see the entire club.

Soon, it would be my turn as the roamer, and I was not looking forward to it. It's my least favorite security position. You can only see what's in your immediate vicinity. If shit breaks out somewhere else in the club, getting there in time to help is almost impossible. Not to mention having drinks sloshing on you, people bumping into you, and idiots trying to start shit.

Roaming is the worst, especially as a female security guard; someone always wants to try me. That's their mistake.

I scan the club, my eyes settling on the stranger at the bar. She's still there with her companions. She's leaning back against it with a drink in hand as she watches the dancefloor with a hint of a smile on her lips. It doesn't reach her eyes, though. Her friend in the dress leans over and whispers in her ear; whatever she says makes the smile light up her green eyes.

Shaking my head, I adjust my jacket and earpiece again.

"Gray, you're roaming. Go ahead and start your laps when Marcus reaches you."

"Copy."

Now where the fuck is Marcus?

He's always the last one to rotate onto the back platform, and we have the same rotation almost every night. Somehow, he still manages not to be where he's supposed to be at the right time. He might be the worst.

"Yo, sorry, I got caught up on the edge of the dancefloor." He gives me a wicked smile and wiggles his eyebrows as he climbs the stairs.

"Dude, you can't use the same excuse every time," I say back with a straight face while struggling to hold my smile. Marcus is a pain in the ass, but he's hilarious and one of the only people on the team that I would entrust with my life.

Climbing the last step, he gives me a playful shove, and my smile breaks loose.

"Come on, kid, give me a break. I gotta bust a move occasionally to loosen up these old bones."

Shaking my head, I start down the staircase. Shouting, "Enjoy the view!" I give him the finger as I hit the floor, turn to my right, and walk towards the bar.

Instead of keeping an eye on the dancefloor and the corners, I immediately seek out the glimmering, dark navy jumpsuit, and strawberry blonde hair.

She's still at the bar, so I'll walk past her as I make my rounds and hopefully get a better feel for why she's at the club. Usually, I wouldn't care, but the fact that she has security with her keeps me coming back. She needs to rethink if she's here for business or to cause trouble. If that's the case, she must not realize whose bar she's in.

Dimitri doesn't tolerate any business going down in his club unless it's *his* business. If you're unfortunate enough to be caught, there's a good chance you won't go home that night or any other night. I'd heard of people missing from Club Midnight after Dimitri "played" with them.

Dimitri has a thing for knives, and one of his passions is seeing how much pain he can elicit from someone without them losing consciousness. It's something I have witnessed and experienced first-hand.

CHAPTER 2

Hannah

Jesus, how did I let Cassie talk me into this?

I wouldn't say I like clubs. I'm not one to go out dancing or anything like that. I'd rather be home with a good book and some warm tea. Yet here I am, at a club, after midnight and in a jumpsuit that makes breathing difficult. It's just not my scene. I hate everything about this, and have no idea how I let Cassie talk me into this or how she got James and Kee to go along with it too.

I've had a rough couple of days at work, and the next thing I know, my best friend and bodyguards are taking me to a local club. Cassie assured us that it was okay and that she knew the club well. Kee and James felt confident in keeping me safe while we were here. I'm pretty sure that going to nightclubs in the seedy part of town is against the rules. Especially seeing how someone has been trying to kill me for several months.

Kee is one of the funniest and kindest people that I've ever met in my life. It's no wonder she became a bodyguard. She's made for it in more than one way. She's strong and caring, but best of all, her sense of humor has a way of calming people down when needed the most. Not to mention she's the exact opposite of James.

Where Kee is humorous and caring, James is icy and critical. I don't know if I've ever heard him tell a joke or even laugh. There's a sadness in him that I can't seem to understand, and he won't share anything about himself. He won't even share how he likes his coffee. He's cold, but Kee softens his blunt edges when he's with her.

I think that's why they are such great partners. They balance each other.

I have complete confidence in them but can't help but feel on edge, not only because of what happened recently but also because I try my damnedest to avoid large, loud crowds, especially when alcohol is involved.

I don't know what Cassie hopes to accomplish tonight, but if dancing is what she has in mind, she is dead wrong. I don't dance, and I don't enjoy drinking much. This is not my definition of a fun night, not at all.

"What do you want to drink?" the surly tattooed bartender yells at Cassie and me as he finishes pouring a drink for a clearly intoxicated young woman.

"I'll have a white wine!" I yell over the thumping electronic dance music.

"No! She'll have a whiskey. Neat. We both will!" Cassie yells, nudging me with her bare shoulder. She's in a dress that has to be held up by magic. It's so tight and strapless I have no idea how she got it on or how she's keeping it on. Only Cassie could look great in scrubs and a dress meant for supermodels.

The bartender returns with our drinks and puts them on the sticky bar. Cassie pays before I can even offer. Turning, she hands me one of the glasses of amber liquid and takes a drink of the other.

"Ah, now that's what I'm talking about! Tonight is definitely not a wine night! Come on, Hannah, relax a little and enjoy the music! I know you love this type of music whether you'll admit it or not!"

Taking a deep breath, I lean back into the bar with my drink in hand. Cassie is right; I do love EDM. There's something extraordinary about getting lost in the beat and the rhythm of a good club mix.

Cassie is already dancing and bopping around to the music as she stands beside me. I know she's dying to get out on the dancefloor.

"Hey! Why don't you go and dance? I'll watch your drink!" I give her a smile and an awkward thumbs-up to encourage her to go dance.

"Are you sure? I don't want to leave you alone."

"I'm fine. I have Kee and James here with me." I hitch a thumb in their direction and follow Cassie's eyes as she looks from Kee and James to the dancefloor.

"Okay, I'm going to go, but like just for a song or two!"

Cassie dances her way away from the bar and is immediately swallowed up by the other patrons of Club Midnight.

With Cassie gone, Kee settles on one side of me and James on the other. Both of them are attempting to act casually and are failing miserably.

Maybe it was a mistake coming here. I feel uncomfortable for many reasons, but Midnight's vibe is off. It seems more sinister than your typical nightclub, where shady things go down. It's seedy, and there are too many dark corners for my liking. Too many places where you can get into trouble. Kee picks up on my discomfort.

Leaning in, she whispers, "Do you want to leave? Is this too much?"

"No, we're here already, so we should at least finish our drinks." I'm trying to be nice because I know Cassie did this for me, and Kee and James went along with it because my already reclusive life had become even more so over the last several months.

"Hey, love, come dance with me!" I look at the tall, muscular man with gelled-back hair in front of me as his drunken words slam into my face at the same time as his stagnant breath hits me. I'm trying not to wrinkle my nose as he moves towards me, blatantly looking my body up and down before looking me in the eyes.

"Sorry, no thanks. I'm just enjoying my drink with friends to-night." I realize my mistake immediately as he moves closer to me. I was too nice.

Kee shifts closer to me, angling her body towards the man as he moves closer. James does the same. I can feel the tension in their bodies as they prepare to react. I also know that I specifically asked them not to scare everyone away tonight, so they may be waiting for me to say something before they make a move.

"Come on! You look like you wanna dance!" He moves closer as I try to disappear into the bar behind me. Kee and James start to move towards the sweaty, drunken guy, pushing me behind them when a voice cuts through the music as if it wasn't even there.

"I believe she said she didn't want to dance." The voice comes from behind the man and is cold and dark. My eyes widen as the man moves back and turns towards the voice behind him.

She is tall, around 5'8" or 5'9", wearing a tailored suit and jacket with a skinny black tie, a white dress shirt, and black dress shoes finishing it. Her hair is dark brown, maybe black. I can't tell in the club's light. It's styled as an undercut and a bit longer on top. It's wavy and a bit unkempt.

Even with the suit on, which is a men's cut, I can see that she's muscular. She's not too firm but definitely not soft, and I can see the outline of her biceps through her suit jacket. She doesn't have what many would think of as a feminine body.

My mouth might be open.

We all look at her, shocked by her appearance.

Who is she? Does she work here?

I look up at her as the man steps to the side, quickly removing himself from the situation. She's got a scar running down the left side of her face from just above the eyebrow, almost to the corner of her mouth. It's still a dark pink and slightly puckered, making me think it's not too old of an injury. I'm still looking at her scar when she speaks again.

"Everything good here?"

I look down, embarrassed. She definitely caught me staring at her. I look up, meeting her gaze. I feel the heat creeping up my neck, cheeks, and ears. Nodding, I tuck a strand of hair behind my red right ear. A bad habit I picked up in medical school that I can't seem to shake. One of the only things that I still do that gives away how insecure I can be. I thought it would be something I would grow out of as I got more confident in my skills as an ER doctor, but it seems to have stuck with me.

The woman standing in front of me radiates strength and confidence from the set of her lips to how she stands with her legs spread and squared. Perfectly balanced and ready to act if needed.

Goosebumps rise on my arms, and my breath hitches. A familiar but lost fluttering in my stomach and tightness in my chest makes me raise my eyes to meet her gaze.

Her eyes are electric blue, and the club's lights magnify and bounce off them like the sun off the ocean's crystal blue water.

The music seems to fade around me as I look at her, and I know she can see the red creeping up my skin, a brand that always gives me away. But in this brief moment, looking into her eyes, I stop caring about how embarrassed and uncomfortable I am. I forget that I'm in a club, and most importantly, I forget that someone is trying to kill me.

CHAPTER 3

Gray

repeat myself, "All good here?" Looking from one person to the next, waiting for someone to answer.

My mystery woman nods again as her eyes glance over my body before landing on my face. Her flushed skin gets redder as our eyes meet. Perhaps because it's undeniable, she's checking me out, or maybe she's not as confident as I first thought.

The male bodyguard moves forward, placing himself more firmly before her. "Yeah, everything's good here. We would have handled him if needed." I give him a once over, my left eyebrow arching and lips pressing together. I feel the skin around my scar pulling with the arch.

"Sure, maybe next time, move a little faster." He needs to know that they should be better at doing their jobs, especially in this club.

Her bodyguard decides to puff up his chest and step forward until he is entirely in front of the mystery woman.

"I think we'll be able to handle it. Why don't you go about your business." I'm about to respond when Marcus' voice slides into my earpiece.

"Gray, we need you over by the entrance. There's a scuffle be-tween the doormen and some idiots." I instinctively reach up to my earpiece, pushing it into my ear more so I can hear. Their eyes track my hand movement clocking the earpiece as I lower my head as if that will help me hear better.

"Copy, I'm on my way." I look around her bodyguard into her green eyes. "Enjoy the rest of your night." With a slight nod, I'm off, going through the sweaty bodies that pack the dancefloor.

Fuck, she's beautiful.

I can't help but think about her eyes, freckles, and flushed skin as I quickly weave through the crowded dancefloor. This is not the time nor the place to be catching feelings. I need to get it under control.

Focus, Gray.

I'm late to the party as usual for a roamer. Breaking through the cluster of dancers, I approach the club's entrance. Everything appears to be okay. I look for Luke and receive confirmation that everything's good in the form of a nod and thumbs up, followed by a wide, goofy grin. He's so damn foolish and awkward. I can't help but give a lopsided grin in return.

I have no idea how he ever got a job working security here. He has the right background as former military but is the clumsiest person I've met. That's why we keep him at the door. There's less need to walk around, which means fewer opportunities for his clumsiness to get him into trouble. Luke is a young soul, a first-timer, and not as jaded as the rest of us. His youthfulness and humor are his best qualities, but they get him into trouble, especially when off duty.

I give him the usual annoyed look, rolling my eyes dramatically, and pick up my route from the door, walking to my left towards the restrooms at the club's front, another familiar spot to find people up to no good. It seems relatively quiet tonight. Maybe it's slowing down. It's past midnight, after all, nearly 2:00 AM, our closing time.

Even knowing that the calm won't last, there's a magic that settles over places like Midnight. People throw their inhibitions and worries aside and let the music drive them. For however long they're here, they're free. Free from the outside world, at least, but not from Midnight. Not from the greed and lust of Midnight. It swallows them all before spitting them out, drained and exhausted yet exhilarated, back out on the streets of reality.

They become hooked on Midnight, coming back every weekend to indulge again and again. It's an addiction that they can't kick.

As I walk on the edge of the dancefloor, I can't help but drift back to her. I am more than intrigued. I feel drawn to her, and I'm not sure why. Thinking of her makes my heart beat faster, and something in my chest feels tight.

What the fuck is this?

CHAPTER 4

Hannah

I can still feel the heat on my face even though she's no longer around.

She was scary, intimidating, and fascinating. I can't believe I got so flustered, and my face got so red. I'd love to blame it on the whiskey, but I've barely had any of it. I'm glad Cassie didn't witness this. She would give me hell for weeks if she had. I have a feeling once we get back to my house, Kee will be sure to bring it up.

I turn around to face the bar looking, hoping for anything to take my mind off the tall woman in black and mocking eyes of Kee.

"What was that all about?" Kee asks, turning with me and leaning in close. James is still puffed up and looking around like he owns the place.

"What do you mean?" I'll downplay it and see how much she will push it.

"You know what I'm talking about. You completely froze when tall, dark, and angry stepped in. Not to mention I've never seen your face get so red." As Kee speaks, her face morphs from a curious look to a shit-eating grin.

Here we go.

"I have no idea what you're referring to. Everything was totally normal." I can feel my face turning red again, and I take a large swig of my drink. It doesn't go down smoothly, and I cough at the burn.

Kee laughs at my expense as I cough on the burning golden-brown drink. Whiskey is not something I would pick for myself. I prefer white, sparkling or rosé wine. Whiskey is too rough for me, too dark—just another thing I let Cassie talk me into tonight.

I've learned my lesson now and won't return to this club or have this drink again. I'll never be able to show my face around here after tonight.

I sit my drink down, ignoring Kee completely. A part of me wants to bolt out of the club and escape everything. But I also want her to come back and walk past just once more.

Would I even do anything if she walked past again?

"Want me to go ask for her contact information?"

"Ugh, Kee, stop. It's not funny." I take another drink and shove Kee softly. James takes up his post on my other side and seems utterly oblivious to the pain that Kee is putting me through.

"This is why you came out. So, you could blow off a little steam and relax a little bit. Maybe all you need is a spin around the dance-floor with that one."

"First of all, I didn't want to come. This was Cassie's idea, and you both agreed to it. Which, mind you, I will remember. I wanted to stay home and have a nice quiet night. Instead, I'm here at a club where I don't want to be, making a fool of myself!"

Kee laughs, and I swear I see a slight smile on James' face out of the corner of my eye. Kee puts her arm around my shoulders, pulling me into a half hug. I know they're teasing me and trying to help me have a good time, but I want to leave. It's late, and the whiskey is starting to hit me. I can feel a warm fuzzy sensation slowly passing through my body, starting in my chest and working outwards through my limbs. My cheeks feel warm and tingly. Sleep sounds fantastic right now.

"Can we just get our coats and call it a night, please?" I put just enough whine in my voice to clarify that I'm ready to go.

"Alright, alright. I'll go get our coats." James finally concedes and heads off into the crowd.

> "Hey, I hate to do this to you, but I'm heading out with someone. I'll see you at work, have a good night and relax!"

Cassie's text comes through as James walks away. I love her to death, but this is definitely one of her toxic traits. It's just like when we were in school. Cassie drags me out somewhere and then leaves me to fend for myself. At least now I have Kee and James.

> "Have fun and be safe!"

I hit send while looking around the club, hoping to see the female bouncer again before we leave. Instead, an older man with cold dark eyes standing on the staircase platform catches my eye.

The hair on the back of my neck stands up as he focuses on me. His gaze is one of a predator, cold and dangerous.

"Where the hell is James with our coats?" Kee asks, and I snap my eyes away from the man on the platform. We both turn away from the bar, hoping to see James approaching us, but the flashing lights reflecting off the sweat-covered bodies are all I can see.

And her.

My heart rate immediately jumps up a couple of notches. I need to calm down so that I don't turn red again. Should I go up to her? What would I even say?

"Holy shit, there's tall, dark, and scary! She came back around." Kee elbows me gently, pretending not to notice that I'm hyperventilating.

I turn around only to come face-to-face with the man from the platform. I inhale sharply at his sudden appearance.

"I couldn't help but notice you talking to Gray earlier. That's impressive. Gray doesn't talk to a lot of people." His voice doesn't match his demeanor. It's soft and smooth and reminds me of the color of my whiskey.

"I don't know who you're talking about." I haven't talked to anyone except for... Oh no.

I glance up sharply just in time to see him reach for his earpiece.

"Gray, can you come to the back bar, please? There's a situation." I can hear a hint of teasing, and his once terrifying eyes seem to get lighter.

He gives me a full-on smile as he tilts his head to the side and down, similar to how she had done earlier. She must have responded. My stomach does a little flip, and I don't know if it's from the whiskey or the nerves. Kee leans towards the stranger giving him a wicked smile once she realizes what he's done.

I need to escape.

CHAPTER 5

Gray

just checked the back bar, and nothing was happening, so why is Marcus asking me to return there now?

I'm looking forward to the end of my shift tonight. I've got a nice quiet apartment and a nice glass of whiskey waiting for me once I'm out of here.

Pressing my earpiece, I turn around and walk back to the bar. "I'm on my way."

He better be fucking with me because the last thing I want to deal with right now is some asshole that won't pay their tab or has an issue with the bartender. I do not have the patience for it tonight. I glance over to the platform only to see it empty.

Shit, if he's left his post, something serious must be happening at the bar.

I pick up the pace, walking quickly. Marcus is always calm under pressure, so who knows how serious the situation might be.

I stop when I break through the dancers and see Marcus. There he is, standing behind the bar with a devious grin. He's standing right behind the woman in the navy jumpsuit and her security.

That son of a bitch.

I can tell by his smile what the game is. He must have seen our interaction earlier. I'll make him pay for this later.

After pausing for a moment, I keep walking towards Marcus. I can feel a scowl creeping over my face as he looks at me. I can't help but narrow my eyes at him in disapproval.

The last thing I need is for his smart ass to be my wingman. Everything is a joke with him. If I want to pursue someone, I can damn well do it on my own without Marcus making it into a joke.

I try to act casual as I nod to our bartender, Davis, making my way to where Marcus has set up shop. He's avoiding my scowl as I navigate through the crowd and to the bar, using the side door to get behind it.

Marcus is talking freely with the female security guard. The surly male security guard doesn't seem to be around. The mystery woman is glancing between Marcus and me. She's nervous. It radiates off her in waves.

I come to stand next to Marcus and give everyone a tight smile and nod. I don't know what to do with my hands, so I put them in my front pockets to avoid crossing them or standing with them clasped behind my back.

"Let me introduce my friend, Gray. Gray, this is Kee, and this young lady is Hannah, pronounced Hann*aaah*!" I can almost feel the laughter bubbling off Marcus as he makes the introductions making sure to over-pronounce the "ah" in Hannah's name.

"Don't let Gray's face scare you. She always looks this way. Even when she's having a good time." He slaps me hard on the back while throwing Kee a wink.

What the fuck has gotten into him?

I open my mouth to give him some shit back when my earpiece explodes with voices. Marcus and I reach for our earpieces to make sense of the overlapping voices.

"Sounds like something's going on at the door," I say, looking at Marcus. "Stay here while I check it out. You might want to get back to your post before anyone notices." I point to the empty platform as I start away.

"Sounds like a good one, radio if you need backup."

As I break into a jog, I throw a thumbs up in Marcus' direction. This fight could not have broken out at a better time. It saves me from making an ass out of myself and Marcus from having weeks of material for his jokes.

I break through the dancefloor to find myself in the middle of at least a ten-person brawl. It is absolute chaos. In the dark, it's hard to tell who's fighting, who's trying to get the hell out, and who's coming at me. I have no idea how or why the fight started, but I don't care. My job is to stop it and get everyone out of the club. I don't give a shit if they keep fighting outside; just don't do it in here.

I jump into the fray, grabbing the first guy by the back of his collared shirt and pulling him backward and off-balance so he has to stop swinging to catch himself from hitting the floor.

"Fuck off!" I shout at him as he hits the floor. He's a big guy, much bigger than I am, and I know if I let him get to his feet, I'll have a tough time wrangling him. Snarling, he pushes his black greased hair out of his face and goes to get up. His eyes flash with anger, and I know I've got a few options, let him up and have him come at me again, or take the opportunity I have right now with him sprawled on the ground to drive my point home through his thick skull. I put my foot on his chest, bend close, and reiterate that he needs to fuck off.

His drunken ass seems to get it this time and, hauling himself up from the floor, he stumbles out of the front door and into the cold night air. Turning, I similarly grab the next idiot, but before I can pull him off-balance, he turns, swinging wildly. Simultaneously, another drunkard stumbles into my right side, pushing me towards the wild fist.

Fuck, this is going to hurt.

It's not a well-placed punch at all. I take it as a glancing blow to my left cheekbone, but the force of the push, combined with his momentum, causes us to end up on the floor in a tangle of arms and legs. Someone lands another blow as I struggle to get off the floor and find my footing. This one is well-placed and slams into the right side of my face. My teeth snap together and snag the inside of my lip. I hear the click as they connect with the force of his fist, driving them together.

The taste of blood instantly follows the sound, and sparks fly behind my eyelids. I'm on all fours, shaking my head, trying to get my shit together, and spitting blood on the floor when he comes in for another blow.

"What the fuck is your problem?" I shout, sweeping my right leg out, catching his feet, and knocking him flat on his back. He hits hard, his head bouncing off the cement floor. It's the burly guy with overly gelled hair from earlier, the one that was hitting on Hannah. I guess that explains why he has an issue with me.

Standing over him, I see he's even more intoxicated than just an hour ago. Waiting a few seconds, it's clear that he's in no state to get up, and I head back into the main fight to help Luke out as he takes on two large meatheads looking to start some shit. We fight well together, each of us able to anticipate and react to the other's moves. The fight becomes a dance for the two of us, and it takes us a few more minutes to get everyone separated and moved out of the club.

I have a love/hate relationship with doing security at Midnight. I hate dealing with idiots, especially drunken ones. Still, I love being able to knock them around when they get too rowdy. It's an excellent way to get some aggression out and is always justified. I don't enjoy getting sucker-punched in the face, but you've gotta take the good with the bad.

I can feel my face swelling on both sides and know I have a big split in my bottom lip. The left side of my face isn't as sore, but I'll definitely have a bruise on my cheekbone.

Walking to the nearest trashcan, I spit a mouthful of blood into it, wiping the remnants on my suit jacket sleeve. The rest of the team came out in a similar condition. There are split lips, a cut cheek, a bruised rib, and a few cut eyebrows, but nothing major that we're not used to.

"Are you good here, Luke?"

"Yeah, thanks for the assist. I don't know what got them all going, but it escalated quickly."

Luke has a small cut above his left eye that is bleeding slightly and a bruise forming from where he took a well-aimed elbow.

"Make sure you get some ice for your eye and get that cut checked out; you might need stitches," I say, straightening my jacket and fastening the middle button.

Luke nods and swipes at the blood on his brow.

"Can you make it for another thirty minutes until we close?" I ask, taking a step closer to look at his eyebrow.

"Yeah, I'm all good. Andrew and Connor are here, so they have it covered if I need to step away."

"Alright, good job." I give him a smile, wincing as it stretches my cut lip and makes it bleed even more.

"Good job, everyone. Closing is in thirty minutes. If anyone needs to step away, let me know."

Giving Luke another nod and pat on the back, I pick up my route, head towards the restrooms, and work my way outside the dancefloor.

I can't seem to stop the bleeding from my lip and need to stop at the bar for a paper towel to staunch the bleeding. Plus, some ice probably wouldn't hurt. Looking up from my blood-smeared fingers, I see Marcus on the platform shaking his head at me.

"Did you forget to keep your hands up?" he says over the comm.

"Fuck you, Marcus," I mumble through my jacket sleeve, covering my lip.

He chuckles as I walk towards him; he's coming down the stairs to meet me.

"Let me take a look at ya, kid." He lifts my chin as I remove my sleeve from my lip. I hear him suck in a breath between his teeth as he looks at the split.

"Damn, you might need to get this sucker glued back together. Did you break any of your teeth?"

"Not this time," I say with a sigh. Breaking your teeth is one of the worst things ever, and I've broken many things.

"Guy fucking sucker-punched me. I didn't even see it coming."

"Come on, let's get ya some ice and see if we can stop the bleeding."

"Shouldn't you keep an eye on things from the platform?" I ask. I'm not completely serious, but I don't want him to get disciplined if the boss sees that he's not at his post. If that happens, there will be worse things than split lips.

"Nah, it's all right. We're closing, and I can watch from the bar." He looks at me and gives me the biggest smile. "Plus, your lady is still at the bar."

"I hate you."

I can't help but smile as he chuckles and pats me on the back. Smiling makes the split open more, making me wince again.

"Don't make me smile. It hurts!"

"Good thing you don't smile very often, then, isn't it!"

I'm still shaking my head at him as we step behind the bar. Davis is there with a bag of ice and a paper towel.

"Saw ya coming my way, figured you probably needed both." He says as he hands them to me.

"Thanks, man." Wrapping the ice in the paper towel, I press the makeshift icepack to my bloody lip.

"What was that all about?"

Marcus and I both turn and find our three guests watching in curiosity. Hannah looks concerned, and her security looks ready to leave. The male guard holding their coats in his arms looks especially peeved to still be at the bar.

"Nothing, just a little scuffle between idiots," Marcus says, giving Kee a brilliant smile.

Of course, Marcus would use this as an opportunity to keep flirting with Kee.

"Was anyone seriously hurt?" It's the first time I've heard Hannah speak with authority since seeing her earlier this evening. Hannah's voice is soft but has an edge to it. I know she's nervous and maybe a bit self-conscious, but there's strength behind her voice that I wasn't expecting. There's much more to Hannah than meets the eye, and I'm even more intrigued than I already was.

"Oh, ya know, there are a couple of bumps and bruises. This one took a nice punch to the face. You should've seen it!" Marcus says, giving my shoulders a shake.

I roll my eyes and shake my head. I can't help but smile and wince at Marcus' antics. He can never take anything seriously.

"I'm not hurt, just a split lip," I say, looking her in her eyes and immediately getting lost in them.

That feeling again; I can't draw a full breath like my chest is tight or my throat is closing. I haven't felt anything like this in a long time. Something that feels innocent, soft, and dare I say, safe.

Hannah breaks contact first, ducking her head. Her cheeks are stained red again as the blush paints her pale clavicle and face.

"I'm a doctor. I could look at your lip if you…um…if you want." She stammers through the offer, and I'll be damned if I don't feel my heart squeeze from the cuteness.

CHAPTER 6

Hannah

"Oh, we wouldn't want to—" the man, Marcus, begins.

"—Sure, that would be great," Gray cuts in, not looking at anyone but me. I see Marcus jerk his head to the side to look at her in surprise. "Would you mind also looking at a few of our other team members?" Gray continues.

I blink, processing what she said. "Sure, I can look at anyone who needs it."

"If you and your *friends* can stay at the bar after we clear everyone out, I'll bring those that need to be looked at back to you." Gray stresses the word "friends," indicating Kee and James, making me think she knows they're my security.

"I'll be here," I say softly, feeling my cheeks getting hot as she gives me a slight smile, wincing a little as she walks onto the floor.

Gray stops next to the bartender, Davis, before leaving. I assume she's telling him we'll stay here a little longer after closing.

"I can't believe I just did that." I draw a deep breath, hold it, and release it along with the tiniest bit of my anxiety.

"Look at you being all bold and shit!" Kee says, nudging me with her elbow and giving me a huge smile. I can't even look her in the eyes. She continues to rib me, chuckling, and looks at Marcus, still behind the bar. He also has a massive grin, and to my complete surprise, Kee and Marcus high-five!

This is so embarrassing.

"Do you two know each other?" I ask, looking from one to the other, incredulous at this seemingly instant friendship that they've formed.

"Great minds think alike, my friend!" Kee says, glancing at Marcus. James has given up on us, and dropping our coats on a bar stool, he resumes his post with his back to us as he watches the crowd. But I know he's listening because even in profile, I can see the slightest of smiles on his otherwise emotionless face.

How did I end up with these two as my security?

The club's atmosphere shifts to disappointment as the music winds down, and the crowd shuffles towards the exit. The air still hums with the energy created by the music and writhing bodies. I'm pondering my existence and how I can escape this situation when the music cuts off, and they announce that the club will be closing in ten minutes.

I guess there is something magical and freeing about the dance-floor. A place where you can let go and let the music take you away. I can see why people enjoy dancing. Maybe, I should try it out sometime, letting go and just letting the beat run through my body.

I watch as the crowd continues to move towards the club's door. I'm kind of surprised by how orderly everyone moves. I smile because they remind me of a zombie horde—all shuffling together towards the same destination, in various stages of undress. Some are looking more aware than others, but all are moving as one towards their goal.

What was my goal tonight?

I'm unsure what got into me or why I volunteered my medical services. Still, here I am—hanging out in the back of a shady club providing off-the-books medical services to bouncers. I feel the tingle in my stomach as the club empties, and I get more nervous about what will happen.

"Oh my God, what the hell am I doing?!"

The panic is setting in now. I'm almost short of breath.

"Chill out. You're a doctor. You've got no reason to be nervous." Kee's whispered words of encouragement do little to boost my confidence.

"How can I be more nervous about a conversation with a stranger than when dealing with a medical emergency?" I mutter more to myself than to Kee or James.

I can see Gray across the empty dancefloor as she talks with the guys watching the club's entrance. About twenty patrons are waiting to get their jackets from the coat check before leaving; after that, I'm sure they'll start coming back seeking medical attention.

"Do you have a medical kit or anything I can use?" I ask, turning to Marcus, who is still shamelessly flirting with Kee. If I focus on their medical needs, I won't be so focused on Gray, and hopefully, I won't be as nervous.

The last of the clubgoers have left. As Marcus walks up, carrying a pretty impressive medical bag, I catch Gray pointing in my direction.

The medkit is almost military grade. I pop it open to see what I'm working with and am pleasantly surprised by the medical supplies available. I could perform minor surgery with everything in the bag.

This is impressive. I can work with this.

"Hi, Gray said someone here could check out my eye?"

"Yup, this is it. I'm Hannah, and I'll be your doctor tonight," I say, turning and putting on a friendly smile.

"Hi, I'm Luke. I got clocked and split my eyebrow earlier."

Luke is an impressive specimen. He's at least 6'2" tall and has a swimmer's body, sandy blond hair, and a chiseled face. If I were still the confused young woman I was years ago, I would have flirted with him, hoping to get his attention and validation. I'm not that young woman anymore. I need to remind myself of that more often. I'm no longer confused and scared. I know who I am and what I want.

"Sit down, and let's take a look."

Even sitting, Luke is taller than I am, and I've got to stretch a bit to get a good look at his eye. It was a pretty good little cut and was still bleeding.

"You should be fine with a couple of steri-strips to close it. You might have a little scar." I grab what I need from the medical kit to close up the wound above his eye.

"Yeah, I'm good with that." The amusement in his voice makes me pause and look at him more closely. He's got small scars all over his face and hands. Of course, I'm sure someone in his line of work is used to these injuries.

"I'm sure you are." I can't help but smile as I lean back to clean the cut and place the steri-strips with steady well-practiced hands. Even if I'm not at the hospital, I'm in my element now.

"Alright, you're all done. Keep it dry and clean, and let the strips fall off when ready. They should last a couple of days up to a week. Go ahead and send in the next patient."

"Thanks, Dr. Hannah!" Luke replies with one of the biggest and goofiest smiles I've seen in a long time.

I can't help but shake my head and laugh at him as he saunters away. I bet he is a blast to be around.

My next patient is a slightly older man named Patrick. Pat has a cut across his right cheek, but it's like Luke's and only requires some cleaning and a liquid band aid. After Pat, I meet Roco and Jimmy; they also have minor cuts and bruises, but nothing serious.

I send them all on their way with basic instructions on keeping their cuts clean. I don't know why I even do that, though. They have a lot of experience with these injuries and probably know more about caring for them than I do.

I haven't looked at Gray's lip yet and am determined to do so.

I've seen everyone, and they've all cleared out of the club, so only Kee, James, Marcus, and I are there. I don't see Gray anywhere as I look around the empty club. Perhaps, she left without seeing me first. I start placing the medical supplies back in the kit when I hear footsteps echoing through the club.

I turn around, my breath catching in my throat.

Holy shit.

She's taken her jacket off at some point and strides towards me in her black straight-legged trousers and fitted white dress shirt. Gray is no longer wearing a skinny tie, and the top two buttons of her shirt are undone. I can see hints of tattoos on her chest and her forearms as she rolls up her sleeves. I don't know what it is about Gray, but I find everything about her charming and attractive.

Then there's the look on her face. Where a scowl was before is now something else, something slightly predatory. I can't look away as she strides towards me, her electric blue eyes locked on mine. I know I must look stupid right now with my mouth hanging open, frozen with medical supplies in my hands, but I can't seem to make myself move.

"For the love of God, snap out of it, Hannah," I whisper to myself and manage to look away as Gray nears. I turn to put the supplies back on the table I'm using as my makeshift ER.

"Do you have time for one more patient?"

Gray's voice is soft and husky, sending a shiver down my spine. Taking a deep breath to steady myself, I turn to face her.

Whatever I was going to say gets caught in my throat as I turn. Gray is a few feet away from me. I swallow hard; I'm sure she can hear and see it. My heart feels like it will beat its way out of my chest. Thankfully, my ribs are there to hold it in place. I swallow again and lift my eyes to meet hers.

"Just in time. I was about to close up shop," I manage to squeak the words out on a stuttered breath.

Her gaze skims over my eyes, my lips, and my throat. I swallow again and can feel myself breathing faster as she watches me.

"Have a seat." I gesture to the stool behind me.

From the corner of my eye, I see Kee, James, and Marcus walk away to the far end of the bar.

I don't need anyone witnessing me make a fool out of myself.

I gather some supplies from the kit to collect myself before turning to her, sitting on the stool with her legs spread slightly. I almost fall apart at the sight of her sitting there. One eyebrow cocked, and a playfulness in her eyes that wasn't there before.

I step forward and lean in to look at her split lip. I find myself moving closer and standing between her legs before realizing it. She's slouching, so I have a better view of her lip and cheek and don't have to stretch as much. I'm so close to her that I can see the flecks of dark blue throughout her light blue eyes. She also has a dark blue or black ring around her eyes, making them pop.

Her eyes are beautiful, and I am completely lost in them momentarily. Before snapping back to the task, I'm not even sure where I am. I glance down at the supplies in my hands and feel the heat crawling up my neck and settling in my cheeks again. There's no way she doesn't notice it this time.

"Alright, let's look at your lip," I mumbled, avoiding her eyes.

She doesn't say anything as I slowly take my right hand and lift her chin using my index and middle fingers so I can see better. The split runs from the inside, over the top, and through the skin below her lip. It's a nasty cut.

"I think I'll use a liquid bandage on this and probably some steri-strips because of where the cut is."

Gray doesn't respond as I turn back to the kit on the table and pull out the bottle of liquid bandages. As I turn back to her, I notice her balled fists resting on her thighs.

"Are you in a lot of pain?" I ask.

"Huh? What? No, I'm not in pain." Gray follows my gaze to her fists, immediately unclenches her hands, and flattens them. She gives me an almost apologetic look, and the left side of her mouth ticks up in a half-smile. A wince quickly follows.

"Okay, just checking," I say, positioning myself between her thighs again.

If she's not in pain, does she not want me this close to her? Why else would she be clenching her fists like that?

"You can put your hands on my waist if you want," I say jokingly with a nervous chuckle.

Gray's eyes widen, and she jerks her head away from me.

Was I too bold?

I'm unexpectantly overcome with a sense of disappointment, much too strong for the short time I've been around this person. It makes no sense for it to hit me this hard; I don't even know anything about Gray. I don't even know if she's into women.

I'm a fucking idiot.

I can feel my cheeks redden with embarrassment when suddenly her hands gently rest on my waist.

CHAPTER 7

Gray

I'm in trouble.

It's almost like my thoughts are flashing in bright red warning lights in front of me when she turns to look at me. I am close to her, too close, yet not close enough.

I want to be closer.

Hannah is standing between my legs, looking at the cut on my lip, and I'm dying as I try not to touch her. Every muscle in my body is tense as I resist the urge to run my hands up her thighs to her waist.

She leans closer to look at my lip, taking her index and middle finger to lift my chin. I can feel every inch of our flesh where it connects, and I take a deep breath to steady myself.

Her hand drops away as she grabs supplies from the medical kit.

She has no idea what she's doing to me, and I can't tell if she's interested or just the nervous type. All I know is that I get warm when she gets close to me and that I make her nervous.

She glances at my hands as she asks if I'm in pain.

Fuck my hands!

I don't even realize I'm clenching my hands until she mentions it.

I immediately unclench my hands and rub my palms on my pant legs. I'm not in pain from my injuries, at least.

If she only knew what she was putting me through right now.

She moves to stand between my legs again, closer this time. She reaches up with her left hand to lift my chin again, placing her whole hand on my cheek and her thumb just under my chin.

She mumbles something about my hands on her waist that my completely distracted brain can't seem to fully process. My body seems to understand her, though, and I'm jerking back to look at her as I'm still computing what she said.

Her cheeks are getting red again, and for a moment, I swear it looks like she might cry.

Something inside me snaps, and I can't stop myself from lifting my hands and resting them on her waist. I know it's bold and that I might cross a line, that she was probably joking when she said that I could. But I want her to feel steady. I don't want her green eyes to be sad or for her to look so disappointed. I just want to hold onto her.

She stops applying the liquid bandage and looks down at my hands on her waist. Her fingertips against my cheek soften. Her hand feels more like a caress and less clinical. She looks back at me, her thumb moving from below my chin to the lower edge of my bottom lip.

Her pupils dilate, and her lips part as her eyes run over my lips, down my throat, and back up. She swallows hard before leaning in closer, glancing from my lips to my eyes beneath her eyelashes. My grip tightens on her waist as she leans in. Her body settles against mine.

This feels right. *She* feels right. I want to stay exactly like this for as long as possible.

Hannah's left hand settles against my right cheek, running her thumb across the cut on my lip. I flinch slightly at the pain.

"The bandage is dry," Hannah whispers. I swallow hard, the tightness in my body growing with her closeness. Her face is only inches from mine, and I can feel her breath brushing my lips.

I want to kiss you.

"No kissing." I blink and move my head away slightly.

Did I say that out loud?

"No kissing," she says again, "for at least 3-5 days."

"Right," I manage to push the word out even though I'm unsure if I'm breathing right now.

"I'll put a few steri-stripes on your cut to keep it closed."

I nod and wait for her to move away to grab what she needs from the table. But she doesn't move right away. Instead, she brushes her fingertips across the bruise on my left cheekbone.

"You'll need to ice this and your lip." Her voice is soft, almost inaudible, as her fingertips and thumb caress my cheek and split lip.

I feel my eyelids flutter as I try to keep from closing them and leaning into her touch. I can't seem to speak around the lump in my throat, so I simply nod.

She leans back, reaching for the bandages on the table without removing herself from my grasp.

It's as if she doesn't want to let go, like she wants to stay connected for as long as I do.

My grip on her waist tightens, and I feel warmer. I breathe harder as she leans into me again to apply the bandages to my lip. She smells like vanilla and sun-kissed skin. She reminds me of warmth and sunshine.

Her right hand rests on my chest, and I know she can feel my heart pounding.

"Good as new," she whispers.

Her cheeks and neck are flushed, but I know it's for a different reason this time.

Neither of us moves.

My eyes are drawn to her lips as she parts them. I can feel her chest rising and falling with every rapid breath. Her hand is still on my face, her thumb resting just below my lip. I slide my left hand to the small of her back to pull her closer.

"Hey! Hannah, hello! We need to leave."

The shout from across the room breaks the connection, and we drop our hands quickly. As if we were teens caught in the act.

She backs away from me. Her hands immediately tuck her loose hair behind her ears. I clear my throat and clasp my hands together as I remain seated on the stool.

My hands feel cold and empty without her in them. The places that she touched feel bare. The feeling of her skin against mine is a permanent mark that I can't remove or forget.

"I'll just, um, I'll just leave this here if that's okay?" she says, pointing to the medical kit.

"That's fine. I'll take care of it," I say softly.

Her bodyguards are walking over with Marcus trailing behind them. Marcus and Kee have shit-eating grins on their faces, and the other one, James looks like he wants to beat the shit out of me.

I had entirely forgotten that they were even here.

Marcus is going to give me so much shit for this.

"Alright, if you two kids are done fooling around, it's past Dr. Winters' bedtime," James says, glaring in my direction.

Hannah blushes and won't make eye contact with me as she puts her coat on. I'm still sitting, trying to act unbothered because her posse just busted us. I can't help but glance at Marcus as Kee and James move towards Hannah.

Marcus waggles his eyebrows at me, and I roll my eyes.

"Thanks for the medical assistance," Marcus says, stepping up to Hannah. "It was a pleasure meeting you, and we appreciate the help."

She gives Marcus a full bright smile that makes my chest feel weird. It's the first smile I've seen from her tonight that has reached her eyes. She's brilliant. I want her to smile at me like that.

"I'll walk you all out," I offer, standing up and gesturing towards the side door.

Hannah's smile quickly fades as she looks towards me, and she immediately looks anywhere else but at me. I can tell she's embarrassed at being caught, and every fiber of my being wants to gather her in my arms and tell her that it's okay.

I walk them over to the side door and unlock it. "Are you parked close to the club?"

"We're just around the corner," Kee responds, stepping out the door first before motioning for Hannah and James to follow.

I follow them out, closing the door behind me.

"What are you doing?" James asks.

"I'd like to ensure you all get to your vehicle safely. An extra set of eyes can't hurt, right?"

James and Kee look at each other before Kee responds, "Sure, it's fine."

James takes point while Kee and I walk on either side of Hannah.

I put my hand on the small of Hannah's back to guide her as we walk. It's partially out of habit and partly because I miss the feeling of her.

Her eyes dart everywhere as we exit the alley and start down the sidewalk. I can feel the tension radiating off of her. She's terrified. There is definitely something going on. Hannah is scared shitless and has security. It doesn't make any sense.

I take a second to glance at her, pressing my hand into her lower back a little harder, trying to reassure her that she's safe. She went from being flushed and alive in the club to being so pale that her freckles stand out against the starkness of her skin. I feel the tightness in my chest again.

Shit, something must have happened to her.

The tension in my chest grows as I ponder what could have caused this. The need to protect her is almost overwhelming as we approach a dark sedan parked at the end of the block.

"This is us," James says, unlocking the vehicle and opening the back door for Hannah.

She steps forward to get into the vehicle.

"Wait, I'd like to see you again. That is if you'd like to see me also." The words leave my mouth before I can stop or think about it too much.

"Yes," she answers quickly with an even quicker smile.

I must look shocked because Kee chuckles softly as James looks on with disinterest and seems disgruntled.

"Great, um, well, I'll give you my number, and you can reach out when you are ready." She reaches into her small bag, pulls out her phone, and hands it to me.

I open her contacts and quickly enter my information. I glance at who is at the top of her recent contacts as I do so.

I wonder who Marshal is?

"I'm under Gray Alexander," I say, returning the phone to her.

"It was nice meeting you tonight, Gray Alexander," she whispers, her eyes lingering on my lips long enough for me to start forward.

Leaning in, I reply, "Likewise, Dr. Hannah Winters," with a lopsided grin.

Hannah lets out a small huff of air as I slowly lean back. She smiles and shakily gets into the vehicle. Kee following closely behind her, gives me a thumbs up, and James slams the door behind them. He gives me a stern look before walking around the front of the vehicle and getting in the driver's seat.

I stand on the sidewalk's edge until their vehicle is out of sight. Enjoying the feeling of my heart beating against my chest.

CHAPTER 8

Hannah

I can't stop smiling as we drive back to my house, replaying the night in my mind. This was the last thing I expected to happen tonight.

"Thank you both for agreeing to let me go out tonight," I say softly to Kee and James as I struggle to keep my smile contained.

"See, we told you it would be good for you. I didn't think you'd walk away with someone's number, but good for you, girl!" Kee says, beaming at me.

I smile back at her, laughing. I feel giddy with happiness, which I haven't experienced in many years.

"I don't know what came over me tonight. That's the boldest that I've ever been in my life!"

"Shit, we gotta get you out more," Kee says, looking at me in the rearview mirror.

I smile at her in return, and turn to look out the window. If only that were something that I could do. I don't go out as it is because of my work schedule, and now with everything that's been happening, going out and taking time for myself has been the last thing on my mind.

Tonight was the first time I've been out in over a year. Typically when I go out, I enjoy a nice dinner and some wine, so I can sit back and relax and not deal with people. I do enough of that at work. This was good, though. Tonight was good.

I look down at my phone at Gray's contact information, which glows at me from the screen.

"Will you call or text her?"

I turn to Kee, contemplating her question. "Yes, I think I will."

Her smile makes me feel even happier. I know that my father hired Kee and James to keep me safe and that they're technically his employees, but right now, they're my friends and happy for me.

CHAPTER 9

Gray

Walking back into the club, I expect to see Marcus waiting for me with one of his infamous smiles. To my complete surprise, he doesn't seem to be around. I guess he decided that he'd tortured me enough for one night.

Christ, it's almost 3:00 AM.

I take a lap around the club, making a final lap. I glance at the boss' office to ensure the light is off. Dimitri comes and goes as he pleases, and we try to keep an eye out for him and his muscle, Vlad. We know when Vlad's around, the boss is around and tighten up our efforts a bit.

I didn't see Vlad tonight, which is good. It means Dimitri likely took the night off. I relax because Marcus will likely get away with his antics tonight. I don't want Marcus to get in trouble for leaving his post. Not to mention the fight and Hannah staying after to tend to everyone. If Dimitri saw any of that, it would result in discipline for all of us. The boss is brutal and likes to keep his employees in line through fear rather than leadership. He is dangerous, and it's best to stay as far off his radar as possible.

Closing the alley door behind me and locking it, I set the alarm system as I head home for the night. Walking around the club to the back, I climb onto my bike, start the engine, and put my helmet on. I can't help but think about her, about Hannah. The way my hands still burn with her touch, the way her face flushes when she's nervous, the feel of her hands on my face.

I wonder what it would feel like to have her body wrapped around mine on the back of my bike?

My heart starts to beat faster just thinking about it. I need to be careful with this one and go slow. Hannah seems delicate, and there's something else going on. Otherwise, she wouldn't need security. I need to get to the bottom of that first.

Don't get ahead of yourself. She has to call you first.

I pull into my driveway, kill the lights, and scold myself for thinking so much about someone I know nothing about. I can't let her take up too much space. I need to stay focused on the job; the last thing I need right now is to be distracted. I have too much riding on this to fuck it up over a girl.

Just stay focused, Gray.

My phone vibrates in my pocket as I unlock my door. My heart skips a beat.

The name staring up at me from the illuminated screen isn't the one that I'm dying to see. No, it's Roy, another one of Dimitri's henchmen, and there's only one reason he would be calling this late.

Dimitri wants something.

"Hey, Roy."

"Gray. The boss needs you at the warehouse for a meeting. Come prepared."

"Copy, I'm on my way." Fuck. This is the last thing I need tonight. If Roy asks me to come armed, there's a good chance that whatever meeting Dimitri is having will go south.

Entering my apartment, I grab my sidearm and head back down to my bike. It's best not to make Dimitri wait. I've got no time to let Marcus know what's going on, and knowing I'm heading into a contentious meeting without backup makes my stomach knot.

CHAPTER 10

Hannah

t's six in the morning when the call comes in. I'm needed at the hospital, and I know it must be severe, seeing as I'm not on call. They wouldn't call me in if they had it under control.

Getting out of bed and finding a clean pair of scrubs, I toss my slightly tangled hair into a haphazard pony on top of my head and head towards my bedroom door.

"Kee?" I shout as I head down the hall, and before I hit the top of the stairs, Kee is already halfway up the steps, weapon in hand.

"What! What is it? Are you okay?" she asks, climbing the last few stairs to me.

"Yes, sorry. The hospital called. They need me to come in. I need to leave now."

Nodding, Kee radios James, who I know is out in the car, likely napping as the additional security they've brought in takes the heavy lifting during the night.

"Go for James." His voice is deeper, husky as we pull him awake.

"Hannah has been called into the hospital and needs to leave ASAP."

"Copy. I'm ready when you are."

Kee nods to me, and we head down the stairs and out the front door. I see the other security milling about at either end of my short street. I know there are at least six of them in total, but I rarely see them. Kee and James are the only ones that I interact with, and I'm thankful for that. I can pretend the others don't exist and still feel like a tiny bit of my life is mine.

"We could just walk," I say as Kee ushers me towards the car. "It's only a ten-minute walk." I'm dying to get some air and space, and walking would give me time to get my head right for heading into the hospital at this hour.

"I'm afraid we can't do that, Hannah. We aren't prepared for it. I'm sorry." Kee gives me a sad smile opening the car door for me as she does so.

"I understand." I begrudgingly climb into the car, giving James a stiff smile.

Kee gets in beside me, and I close my eyes, mentally preparing myself as much as possible on the short ride to work.

CHAPTER 11

Gray

kill the light of my motorcycle as I drive up to the warehouse. I have no idea what I'm walking into and don't feel like announcing myself until I have a better idea.

I park a reasonable distance from the door and slowly walk up, sticking to the side, out of eyesight of the windows. I can see that the bottom floor of the warehouse is dimly lit.

Walking up to the building, I stay close to the wall and ease my way to the door, ducking below the windows and keeping quiet to hear what's being said.

"What time is the MarConey family getting here?" Roy asks softly.

"Should be here in ten minutes," Vlad answers, his thick Russian accent making it difficult to hear his words through the old, rusted metal door of the warehouse.

So, this is about the MarConeys and the information that was leaked to the FBI and DEA.

I take a few steps back from the door and am sure to drag my foot and kick some gravel so that it pings off the door, announcing my arrival before I open it.

"Someone's here," Roy mutters softly to Vlad.

I open the door slowly, peeking around the metal, waving my empty hands as I enter the warehouse.

A few portable lights are set up, along with a folding table and two chairs. One on each end of the table. Other than that, the warehouse has been cleared out. It's cold and barren, much like Dimitri's eyes as he looks up at me from the end of the table.

"You're late." Dimitri looks at the gold watch hanging from his wrist.

Bowing my head slightly, I apologize and take my spot next to Roy and Vlad. Dimitri doesn't ask me to attend many of these meetings, so I'm not sure what I'm supposed to do other than stand there and look intimidating.

I glance over at Roy and Vlad, looking at their tattooed hands, and notice that Roy has a new tattoo, a skull.

"You like it?" Roy sneers, waving his hand in front of my face. "Maybe if you get your shit together, you'll get one someday."

"Enough," Vlad snarls, looking between us. Vlad has a variety of tattoos, including skulls and an eagle. I know enough about the Russian mob to know that skulls mean that a person is a murderer, and an eagle is a sign of someone who's an authority figure.

I also know that Dimitri has stars on his shoulders, indicating he's in charge. His hands are clean of tattoos, though.

I glance down at my hands; they're tattoo-less, but I wouldn't say they were clean.

Guilt rings through me as I glance from my hands to the window. It lights up with the headlights of an approaching vehicle.

My guilt quickly turns to a nervous feeling, and I shift on my feet, finding my grounding and preparing for the warehouse door to open. Roy and Vlad seem to do the same next to me.

The door swings open, and the MarConey family walks in. The head of the family, Jordy, leads the way with his eldest son Michael next to him. Following closely behind them are four bodyguards.

Good, we're fairly evenly matched.

"Mr. MarConey, I'm glad you could join me." Dimitri stands up, buttoning his jacket, but not before flashing the hilts of his knives.

"We have much to discuss," Dimitri continues, motioning for Mr. MarConey to sit at the other end of the table.

He obliges Dimitri, and his son takes up the space at his right hand while the guards position themselves across from Roy, Vlad, and me.

"Have you found the rat that got my sons arrested?" MarConey asks. I can hear the venom in his voice, and the distaste radiates off him, making the air tense.

"We have not, but we are still looking into it. I want to keep our businesses in good standing and continue to work with each other." Dimitri rarely asks for anything, and it's interesting to me that he wants to keep working with MarConey so badly. Usually, he would annihilate the family and find a new transporter.

What makes the MarConeys so special?

"I don't think you're trying hard enough. And I think it's because you set it up yourself!" Michael shouts from beside his dad, and I see the switch in Dimitri's eyes. They go from having a little light to them to being dead, shut off.

The atmosphere gets tense as we all shift, preparing for what Dimitri will do next. He dictates how this goes.

Mr. MarConey feels the change, sees it in Dimitri, and knows that his son has messed up. Dimitri can wipe out their entire family if he wants to, and he'll do it without remorse.

"Sorry, I apologize on my son's behalf. His youthfulness gets him in trouble."

Dimitri doesn't move or say anything, and I feel Roy stiffen beside me. I risk a glance at Roy and Vlad and get the sense that shit's about to go down.

Before I can fully prepare myself, Dimitri pushes his chair back, standing he buttons his jacket again.

"This meeting is over," he whispers and walks past the three of us. As he does, I see that he gives Vlad a pat on the arm, which Vlad nods to.

What does that mean?

"Dimitri, wait! We can talk this out! Fuck! You little shit!" MarConey turns, striking his son as Dimitri continues out of the warehouse.

MarConey's guards are so distracted by what he's doing to his son that they don't see Roy or Vlad pull out their weapons until it's too late.

Two gunshots echo through the empty warehouse as the elder MarConey and his son fall to the cold, dusty warehouse floor. Each is done in by a single shot to the head.

I know the shots are coming, but I still jump at the sound and watch as the bodies crumble to the floor, seemingly in slow motion. A noise to my right makes me turn just in time to take a punch to the face. I fall and hit the floor hard, catching most of my weight on my butt and elbows. I scuttle backward as one of the guards continues his pursuit of me.

Vlad is taking on two of the guards, and Roy is engaged with another. I roll to the left as the guard lashes out with a kick that grazes my ribs.

That was close.

I keep rolling and try to stand when a heavy booted foot catches me in the ribs. Black dots dance before my eyes as I feel and hear the impact.

I can't breathe and double over, curling in a ball as the guard drops another kick into my stomach and side.

Managing to gasp in a dusty breath, I grab the guard's foot, only to have red mist suddenly cover me. I freeze, thinking for a moment that I've been shot. My eyes lock with the guard's, and I watch as the light slowly seeps from them, like the blood seeping from the hole in his chest.

I scramble out of the way as he falls to his knees before slumping to the floor. I look up to find Vlad standing a few feet away with his gun still pointed in my direction.

I gulp down another breath, holding my side, "Thanks," I gasp out.

"Pathetic." Disgusted, Vlad turns away, and he and Roy walk out of the warehouse to their car. I'm still trying to get up when they walk back into the warehouse with gas jugs in their hands. They start at the bodies and spread it around, covering everything in the liquid.

Vlad hands me a book of matches.

"So you can do something helpful."

The guilt returns.

I strike a match and watch as it catches the rest of the book.

Walking backward, I flick the matches towards the bodies of the MarConey family.

May they rest in peace.

CHAPTER 12

Hannah

We pull into the empty parking lot of the hospital, and I jump out before Kee or James can make a move.

"Damn it, Hannah, wait!" James shouts after me.

I don't bother answering and keep heading towards the doors of the ER. Walking in, one of the nurses is there waiting for me.

"We've got a multi-vehicle accident coming in. It's all hands on deck. A trucker fell asleep on the interstate and rolled his truck, causing a fifty-car pileup. We're getting around twenty patients, and the rest are going to other hospitals in the area."

I pass her my jacket as she passes me my stethoscope, and I head over to the other doctors on duty. Cassie runs in shortly after I do and stands next to me. She's obviously not wearing her clothes, as the gray sweats are a bit too big, and she's drowning in the shirt.

"Good night?" I whisper, trying unsuccessfully to hide my smile.

"Oh, you have no idea," Cassie whispers back, giving me a wink and smile as the doors to the ER open.

Chuckling, I watch the ambulances roll in and let the chaos take over momentarily before taking the reins and leaning into it.

I follow my patient to exam curtain two and start my workup.

"We've got an open tib./fib., going to need X-ray, Ortho., and MRI. Do we have anyone from Ortho. down here yet?"

"Dr. Katnov is on the way down right now."

"Great, make sure we're on his list of people to see. Let's get fluids going and get to cleaning the wound."

Nurse Grace nods and starts on the fluids while I closely examine the wound. It's a bad break, and she is going to need surgery. The sooner we can get the patient to surgery, the better.

I give Nurse Grace a look to let her know that I'm moving on to the next patient and that she should continue with my orders for our first patient of the night.

Moving over to curtain five, I'm greeted by Nurse Drew.

"What have you got for me, Drew?"

"Dr. Winters, this is Penny. She took a nasty hit to the head when her mom's car was hit from behind."

"Hi, Penny. I'm Doctor Winters. Can I have a look at your head?" The little girl in front of me is terrified, and the C-collar does nothing to help her discomfort.

"Penny, can you move your toes for me? Great! How about your hands? Can you squeeze my hands? Wonderful! You did a great job!"

"Drew, how about we take off the collar, I want a CT, and she will need some sutures for the cut on her forehead. Was mom brought in as well?"

"Next curtain over," Drew says, pointing his chin towards curtain six.

"You're doing great, Penny, and are being so brave. I will leave you with Nurse Drew; he will take great care of you!"

I close the curtain and move to six to find Cassie and two nurses attempting to resuscitate Penny's mom.

"Switch!" I shout, giving Cassie a break and moving to take her place with compressions.

Cassie moves aside, instructing a nurse to charge the paddles to 250.

"Clear!" Cassie shouts as we get a faint rhythm. I stop compressions and step back.

The first shock doesn't do it.

Nor the second.

The third try does it, and we have her back.

Cassie takes it from there, instructing the nurses to get fluids and ordering all the scans to figure out what's happening with Penny's mom.

Before I know it, the ER has a weird calmness fall over it. All our patients have been seen from the car crash and taken to other hospital departments.

I lean against the nurse's station with Cassie.

It's eight in the morning. The last two hours have flown by, and the heaviness of exhaustion kicks in as the adrenaline wanes.

"Great job today, Cassie." I lean my head on her shoulder.

"You too, Hannah."

Kee walks up, with James following closely behind. They've been here the whole time, staying out of the way but close enough that they can jump in to help if something happens.

"You good?" Kee asks.

"Yup, all good. We didn't lose anyone, so today will be a good day."

"Don't jinx us!" Cassie yells, punching me softly in the arm.

I fake that it hurts, laughing along with her.

"Should we go get breakfast?" I ask, looking from my best friend to my bodyguards.

"Hell yeah," Cassie says.

"Good. I want to hear about this boy you went home with!"

CHAPTER 13

Gray

By the time I get back to my apartment from the warehouse, all my adrenaline has faded, and the shakes are setting in.

I've seen and done a lot of shit, but something about seeing someone get shot right in front of me still shakes me to the core.

As I climb off my bike, my legs almost give out, and my stomach turns.

Please, not now.

I stumble through my apartment building and make it to my apartment before nausea and panic fully set in.

I run to the bathroom, throw open the door, and kneel in front of the toilet to be sick. With every heave of my body, my bruised ribs rebel, reminding me that I just got my ass kicked.

I should have done better tonight. I totally blew it. There's no way that Dimitri will keep me on his team if he knows I can't keep up with Vlad and Roy. I need to be on his team. Need to be on the inside.

I heave again and groan at the pain. Once the heaving stops, I lean back against the wall letting the pain subside.

Standing up in my small, poorly lit bathroom, all I can see is red against my pale and clammy skin. My stomach turns again as I make my way to the shower.

I need to get his blood off me.

I don't even wait for the water to warm up before I step under the stream, desperate to clean myself up.

The tightness in my chest suddenly worsens, and I feel the prickling of tears as I relive the night's events.

After tonight I'm not sure if I have what it takes to do what's going to be asked of me.

CHAPTER 14

Hannah

"**D**id you text Gray yet?"

"No, Kee." It's the second time today that she's asked me. It hasn't even been twelve hours since I got her number, and all I've been hearing about today is whether or not I've texted her yet.

"I haven't, and I'm not sure if I will. Give it a break, Kee. You'll be the first person I tell if I text her."

"What do you mean if? How can you not call her?" Kee's voice is progressively getting louder.

"Will you come off it already! I think I just got caught up in the moment last night. Now that I'm not in a club of people grinding on each other, I can think more clearly. I don't think it's smart to get involved with someone for several reasons, the main one being that my life is a fucking mess right now!" Even as I say it, I can feel a weight settling in the pit of my stomach.

"No one's saying you have to get involved with someone. Why not just go out and have some fun? It doesn't have to be anything serious, plus Gray looks like she could show you a perfect time."

Kee gives me a seductive look and raises her eyebrows at me.

"Jesus, Kee, you are unbelievable."

I turn away from her as I feel my cheeks reddening.

She's right, though, and Gray looked like someone who could show me a good time. I wonder if she's more of a "player" or the one-partner-at-a-time type. Not that it matters. I probably won't contact her anyway. I don't need any added stress or drama in my life.

"I'm just saying you should think about contacting her. It won't hurt to go out for a coffee or something and see how it goes."

"Why don't you give Marcus a call? I saw you two exchanging information." I give her a pointed look and am satisfied to see her look embarrassed.

"I would never! That would be super unprofessional of me to do something like that!" She feigns shock, pressing her hand to her chest while giving me a devious smile.

"If I text her, will you leave me alone?"

"I most definitely will." Kee practically jumps for joy as I grab my phone and bring up Gray's contact information.

"Hi, Gray, it's Hannah from the club last night. Are you free to meet for coffee in the next couple of days?"

I feel like my heart will beat out of my chest as I hit send.

"There, I sent her a message. I bet she won't even respond."

"Well, we will just have to wait and see, right? At least you made a move and put yourself out there." Kee pats me on the back as she goes to change shifts with James, who has the glorious duty of sitting in the car outside of my house.

I give her a soft smile as she leaves.

I need this whole situation to be over with already. I want to get back to my life.

"What's the heavy sigh about?" James asks as he steps into my room.

I manage to squeeze a smile out. "Just thinking about my life before all of this started."

"Don't worry, kid. We'll get this all sorted, and then you can return to being the boring doc you were before it started."

"There's nothing more boring than an ER doctor," I say, giving him a genuine smile.

James smiles back at me and checks the street.

"I'm going to be in the living room. Give me a shout if you need anything."

I nod as he walks out. James prefers to watch everything from the living room, whereas Kee likes to be in the room with me. I think that might be because she enjoys the company and needs to talk to someone. Given her penchant for talking, I have no idea how she manages to be alone in the car for hours.

It's nice to have some time to myself finally. It's a beautiful Sunday afternoon. All I want to do is enjoy the sunlight filtering into my room and maybe go for a nice walk later to enjoy the last warmth before winter hits.

I settle into my bay window and curl up with one of my favorite books, my mind drifting as the fall leaves drift on the wind when my phone dings. The sound is jarring and snaps me out of my daydream.

My breath catches in my throat when I see her name on my screen.

CHAPTER 15

Gray

Consciousness flutters in from the corners of my mind, followed by dull pain thrumming through my body.

What time is it?

I crack open my eyes, cringing at the sunlight streaming through my apartment window. Rolling from my side to my back, I take stock of the spots on my body that hurt. Besides my lip and cheekbone, my left ribcage feels rough.

Fuck, my ribs hurt.

I'll have to ice them later today—ice everything.

I run my hands through my hair and over my face, careful not to push too hard on my cheek as I rub the grit from my eyes.

God, last night was a shitshow.

Shaking my head and thoughts of the night before away, I swing my legs over the edge and let my body settle for a moment before I try to move. Leaning to the right, the pain and tightness in my ribs mean the bruising will worsen, but at least they're not broken. They still hurt with even the slightest of movements, though. Taking a deep breath, I stand up again, letting my body adjust before I move. Slow and steady is the mantra this morning. Check that this afternoon.

Shit, it's late already.

I don't know when I got in this morning, but it was probably five or six. The sun started coming up when I was heading back to my apartment.

I shuffle to the bathroom, ready to wash the night and early morning antics off my skin again. I catch a glimpse of myself in the mirror. My short dark hair is sticking up in every direction, and my left cheekbone looks like an egg is trying to explode out of it and is a gnarly black and dark blue color edged in red.

My split lip opened sometime in the night, perhaps during the scuffle. There's dried blood from the cut to the corner of my mouth and down my chin. Turning, I look at my ribs and can see the outline of what will soon be a massive bruise starting.

Then there are the dark smudges under my eyes.

I look like shit.

Sighing heavily, I strip and step into the hot shower. I stand there, letting the heat soak into my sore body, enjoying the feel of the water running down my body. There's something slightly enjoyable about feeling the sting of the water as it washes over my cuts and bruises. The mix of pain and pleasure reminds me that I'm really here. I've gone too far to return if I don't feel anything.

It's tempting to stand in the shower until the water goes cold, but my hunger drives me forward. I wash my hair, finding a large bump on my head where I must have hit it on the club floor last night. Maybe I have a concussion. Washing the rest of my body, I find a few other bumps and bruises from my late-night and early-morning scuffles.

I'm getting too old for this type of shit.

I grab my towel and walk into the bedroom while drying off. I want nothing more than to flop back into bed and sleep. I quickly grab some sweat shorts and a t-shirt pulling them on gingerly. Holding my phone, I head into the kitchen before I can change my mind and cocoon myself in bed for the rest of the day.

I have a brief moment where I feel like I'm going to get in trouble for not being available, and I want to throw my phone across the room. I toss some eggs in the frying pan and power up my phone. I usually don't turn it off, but I did this morning when I got back.

I don't have to work tonight, and I would love not to deal with anyone from work for an entire day, including Marcus. I've got two missed calls from Marcus around 10 in the morning and a text from a number I don't recognize. Thankfully there's nothing from the boss.

I ignore Marcus' voice messages and open up the text.

> "Hi, Gray, it's Hannah from the club last night. Are you free to meet for coffee in the next couple of days?"

A shock goes through my body, starting at the tip of my head and through my core.

She reached out. When did she send this?

The time stamp on her text says 2:15 pm, it's almost 4:00 pm now. Not too long ago, then. For a moment, I forget I have eggs cooking and put my phone down before I respond. I feel uncertain or shaky; maybe, it's hard to explain, and all it took was a text.

Plating my eggs, I grab my phone off of the counter and settle at the kitchen table. I open the text from Hannah again as I shovel eggs into my mouth.

> "Hi, yes. I'm available this evening and tomorrow morning."

Taking a breath, I hit send. I'm not one to say a lot, especially over text. I think it's one of the worst ways to communicate. I'd rather keep it short and simple and have a face-to-face conversation.

I put my phone down and return to my eggs, contemplating what I've just done and if I should have done it. It's too late now; I can't take the text back.

My phone vibrates.

> "Join me at the park on Wilson and Redwood Avenue, around 5, for a walk?"

A walk? Shit, when was the last time I went on a walk for fun?

I don't even know. I look out my living room window, and it looks like a beautiful day outside. It's sunny, and the leaves are bright with fall colors. It will get colder as winter moves in, so this might be the last weekend before the weather changes.

> "I'll see you there at 5."

I type, not thinking or looking at my phone but enjoying the fall colors through the window. I know I shouldn't pursue things with her, and it won't end well. I want her, though, and I need her to like me back. Knowing this, I still can't stop myself from replying. I need her to be mine, even if it's for a brief moment and destroys us.

CHAPTER 16

Hannah

"**S**he said yes!" I almost jump out of my skin as Kee squeals; yes, she squeals in excitement as I show her the text I received from Gray.

"Oh my God, what are you going to wear?" She continues looking me up and down as if my current clothes aren't fit for a walk.

"Um, well, I was just going to wear this," I say, sweeping my hands down my body. I'm in cuffed boyfriend-cut jeans and one of my favorite comfy sweaters.

"No, you have to change. You can't go out like that. Not after what you wore last night! You have to keep her coming back for more!" Kee runs over to my closet and swings it open.

"Kee! I am not getting dressed up to go for a walk. That makes no sense. Also, I'd look like a crazy person! Get out of here, I'll change, but I'll pick my clothes." I grab her playfully and give her a push towards the bedroom door.

"Get out!" I say, pointing.

"Okay, okay, but you should go for something, ya know, casual but sexy."

"Kee, I swear to god, if you don't leave now!"

"I'm going. I'm going!" She winks at me and closes the bedroom door, leaving me with some quiet.

Looking at my closet, I go for a pair of fitted worn jeans, a cream-color tight-fitting cowl neck sweater, and brown knee-high boots.

There. This is perfect. I feel comfortable, and I like the way I look.

I nod my approval and grab my bag heading for the bedroom door. Kee waits outside and nods her approval as I step out of the bedroom.

"That's perfect," Kee says, giving me a huge smile and a thumbs up.

"Hm. Yes, I feel more like myself than I did last night, that's for sure." We head downstairs, and I grab my jacket from the closet as Kee opens the door, signaling to James that we are ready to head out.

James pulls the car in front of the townhouse, and Kee guides me down the steps, her eyes sweeping from left to right. She may be silly at times, but she does her job well, and I've never felt unsafe with her or James as my security.

When my father told me that I needed security, I adamantly opposed having people always watching me and following me around. They've grown on me over the weeks, and I rely on them more now than ever, especially after the first attack.

I try not to dwell too much on the attacks because I don't want them to impact my life or make me scared to live. I want to keep living as I always have, without fear and knowing that people wish me ill. It's hard, though, knowing someone might be waiting for me around any corner.

Kee and James make it a little easier to handle, but sometimes the panic overwhelms me. I would love for my life to return to the way it was before this started. I want to go back to normal.

"What's on your mind?" James asks from the driver's seat.

"Just thinking about life before all of this started," I say, giving him a sad smile. I could have lied and said I was thinking about work or any other number of things, but this is my reality now, and I guess I need to start embracing it.

Kee gives my hand a soft pat. "How about we forget about that for the day?"

Nodding, I gaze out of the window as we approach the park. It's only a few blocks from my house, and I usually would have walked the distance, but it's safer to drive than walk—another downside of people wanting to kill you.

James drops Kee and me off at the corner and drives the car down the block to where our walk will end. They've already scoped this area and know it well, even mapping out the best walking routes from a safety perspective.

Gray doesn't appear to be here yet, so we wait for her and James. This is one of my favorite places to visit since moving out of my apartment downtown. I loved my apartment. It was located close to the hospital, making it much easier, and within walking distance of many great food places.

After the first attempt, my father insisted that I relocate. Luckily, I'd been contemplating purchasing a house and had already been looking when this happened. This whole situation forced me to make many decisions I'd been putting off. Maybe that's the silver lining?

James walks up, joining Kee and me as we wait at the park's gates.

"What if she doesn't show?" I ask, suddenly overwhelmed by nerves.

"None of that. She'll be here," Kee says as she scans the area.

The park is surprisingly busy today, but I suppose everyone has the same idea of getting out one last time before the weather changes.

"Ah, here she comes!" Kee says, pointing with her chin behind me.

My heart ratchets up a few notches as I turn around and see Gray walking down the sidewalk towards us. She's wearing straight-cut jeans, a black V-neck shirt, and a light jacket. Her short hair is messier than last night, and she seems a lot more relaxed in her posture than when she was security at the club.

As she walks closer, I can see that her cheek is very bruised and swollen from last night, and it looks like she has a few new bruises. She also seems to be walking a little tenderly.

As she gets closer, I can see that her lip is swollen more than it should be, and it looks like the bandage didn't stick.

That shouldn't have happened. The glue bandage should have been held together.

She gives me a smile and a wince, and Kee and James nod as she walks up. She has a new, more minor cut above her right eye, just below the eyebrow.

Was she in another fight? When would that have happened?

"Hi, am I late?"

"Right on time," I say with a smile back, "have you been here before?"

"Yeah, but it's been a while. Shall we?"

I nod, and we set off into the park. It really is the perfect day. It's in the low 60s, sunny, and there's a slight breeze that makes the golden leaves shimmer as it runs through them. I love this time of year.

Kee and James drop behind us several steps, so we have some privacy.

"Do you come here often?" Gray asks, looking around the park. The sun catches her eyes as she glances in my direction, highlighting the various shades of blues that run through them.

"Yes, it's one of my favorite parks in the area. There are a lot of different paths and trails that you can take. Plus, the foliage is just beautiful." I smile just thinking about how wonderful the park will be when spring comes. All the flowers will bloom, and the cherry blossom trees will be gorgeous.

For a moment, I forget about how awkward and nervous I'm feeling and forget myself. Turning to Gray, I give her a full smile. "It will be amazing in the spring!"

I almost want to skip with how much excitement I'm feeling and realize that it's not just about the trees but about being outside in the fresh air and meeting someone new. I'm putting myself out there even if this doesn't go anywhere.

She gives me a full smile, and I frown as I see the split widen.

"Did the liquid bandage not hold?"

She reaches up and touches her lip, dabbing the small amount of blood away with the sleeve of her jacket.

"No, it held. I just, um, well. I got into another scuffle last night after closing, and I'm afraid it opened back up."

"Another fight?" I can't keep the surprise out of my voice, "Was it at the club?"

"No, it was something that happened outside of work."

Gray looks away as she says this and doesn't offer any other information. There's definitely more to the story that I want to hear.

"I see. Does that happen a lot with you? Fights, I mean?"

She chuckles softly, looking at me from the corner of her eye. "No, I'm usually in the business of stopping them, not starting them."

"What about you? What kind of doctor did you say you were?"

"Oh, I'm not sure that I did. I'm an ER doctor at McCreary Central Hospital."

"Do you like it?"

"Yes, it's often stressful, but I love what I do, and the team there is amazing."

"Good teams are hard to come by. It's nice that you have that." She smiles again, looking over at me and then down.

We're about halfway down the path I picked for our walk, and I want us to be more casual and closer like we were last night. I guess clubs, throbbing music, and gyrating bodies have a way of helping you be bold.

"How did you get into security?" I ask, hoping to keep the conversation going.

She tilts her head back, momentarily looking up at the trees, "I made a mistake a long time ago, and that one mistake brought me to Dimitri and Club Midnight."

"Dimitri?" I ask, curious to learn more about her.

"Yeah, he's the club owner. He has several clubs around the city, but Club Midnight is their busiest. He took me in when I needed help, and I've been there ever since."

"Do you like it there? At Club Midnight?"

"Hm. Yes and no. I love the guys. Our security team is amazing and has many great people. But did I see myself working security at a nightclub well into my thirties? Absolutely not." She says this with laughter in her voice and a little smirk.

I get lost in her profile, looking at the dimple on her cheek.

I reach up and gently press the back of my hand against Gray's swollen face.

She stops in surprise, looking at me with slightly widened eyes.

"Sorry, it's a habit," I say, removing my hand quickly. "You should put ice on it later, so it doesn't swell anymore." I can feel the heat rising to my cheeks as I walk again.

Gray catches up quickly with a few long strides and keeps pace silently at my side. She says nothing, but I occasionally see her glancing at me as we walk silently.

"It's a good habit, caring," Gray softly says after a few minutes have passed.

I smile and go to turn to her when there's a shout from behind us.

CHAPTER 17

Gray

James shouts from behind Hannah and me as she turns towards me. I can't hear what he's yelling, but it doesn't matter. I grab Hannah by the arm, pull her into my body, and get eyes on someone moving so quickly that they are almost upon us.

I move myself between Hannah and the runner. Her elbow connects with my bruised ribs, knocking the air out of me. I want to double over in pain but focus on the runner coming fast.

James and Kee are both running after him but are too far behind to be of any help. I move Hannah out of the way and prepare myself for whatever may be coming our way.

The runner is wearing a dark windbreaker and black sweats. He also has a hat and sunglasses covering most of his face. I can see his hands as he runs towards us, and he doesn't appear to be making any moves to grab anything out of his pockets or waistline. If he's this close and hasn't pulled a weapon yet, he must be going with a physical approach, which doesn't make sense.

I push Hannah further behind me and move off the path, giving the runner additional space. If I need to engage, I've got room to move now, and Hannah will be out of the way.

The runner is on top of us now, and I hold my breath. The feeling is overwhelming, which is surprising. I'm feeling something I don't usually feel when it comes to a fight. I'm worried, worried about Hannah.

Hannah's fingers dig into my jacket and shirt as she holds tightly to me from behind. I can hear her breathing quicken in fear. I have to protect her; that's my only focus.

The runner…keeps running past us.

Jesus Christ. He's an *actual runner*, not someone out to get Hannah.

I track the runner as he keeps going, turning down a path that leads away from the road and us.

"Alright?" I ask, turning to Hannah. She's still clinging to me even as I turn around, and I can feel her hands shaking through the layers. I reach around, grabbing her hands in mine and pulling her around to face me. Her face is stark white, just like last night, and her eyes are wide with fear.

"It was just a jogger," I say softly, still holding on tightly to her cold, shaking hands. Her hands are whiter than her face from gripping my clothes so tightly. I bring her hands together and clasp mine around them to warm them up. I start to rub them to warm them and soothe her.

"Are you alright, Hannah?" Kee says breathlessly.

Hannah blinks, looking first at Kee and James, then at her hands, and finally up to me. The green of her eyes is electric in the sunlight, and they stand out compared to her pale skin. She shutters and seems to gather herself, even pulling her hands away. I keep a tight grip on them and continue to rub them.

"Y…yes, I'm okay, just a little shaken," she manages through colorless lips. "Thank you for acting so quickly." She looks up at me and then back to our hands.

She breaks her hands loose of mine and throws her arms around my midsection, snuggling in for a tight hug. I want to enjoy that she's hugging me, but this time, without the adrenaline, the pain of her hitting my ribs makes me huff out a breath and hunch over in discomfort.

She immediately pulls back, keeping her hands on me. "Are you okay? Did I hurt you?"

Tears sting my eyes. It takes me a moment, and I put a hand on my ribcage to ease the discomfort. I manage to take a deep breath through the pain that I can only compare to shards of glass dragging over my flesh and bones.

Letting the air out slowly, I whisper, "No, I've got some sore ribs."

"Sore ribs? Let me see!" Hannah grabs my shirt and lifts it before I can stop her.

"Perhaps, we can do this inside somewhere?" James interrupts, stopping Hannah and snapping her out of it.

"Oh, right? Yes, please, I'd like to go home now." Her hands are still holding onto the bottom of my shirt, and I realize she's probably in shock right now, which explains some of her behavior.

"Right, maybe we should get you home." I gently take her hands off my shirt's bottom, keep one of them in mine, and start guiding her towards the vehicle. Kee takes point, and James flanks us. We aren't far from their car, and it only takes a few minutes to get there. Hannah doesn't say anything as we walk. She also doesn't try to take her hand away from mine.

Reaching the car, Kee opens the door, and Hannah steps in.

"Are you coming?" she asks, peering out from the inside of the car.

"Huh?"

"I'd like to take a look at your ribs."

"Oh, uh. Sure, if that's okay with everyone?" I say, looking over to James and Kee. A glance passes between them before James gives me a nod and motions for me to get in the car.

Sliding next to Hannah, James shuts the door behind me and walks around to get in the driver's seat and Kee hops in the passenger's side. As I settle for the ride, Hannah slides closer and reaches for my left hand. I'm surprised, thinking she might still be scared or in shock. I clasp her hand back.

For a moment, I feel like I'm a teen again, riding in the back seat of my parent's car, stealing glances. While secretly holding hands with the girl next door, I insist she is just a good friend. I am always waiting for one of them to catch us in the act through the rearview mirror, but they never do.

It was exciting being on the edge of getting caught and terrifying. If my parents found out I was genderfluid, they would disown me. I also wanted them to find out so I could get it over with and start living my life the way I wanted.

However, they wouldn't figure it out, and I was too scared to tell them. It wasn't until much later that I finally sat my parents down and came out to them. They didn't take it well, which was the last time they spoke to me. I have reached out to them throughout the years, never getting a response.

"We're here," James says from the front, pulling me from my reverie.

"You live close to the park," I say, stating the obvious.

"Normally, I would have just walked there, but Kee and James drive me there with everything going on now."

"What exactly *IS* going on?"

Kee, James, and Hannah glance at each other before James responds, "Let's just get inside first and go from there." He looks at me from the rearview mirror to get his point across.

"Sure, let's start there," I say, sliding towards Hannah's side of the car and climbing out the door that Kee is holding open. I instinctively put a hand on Hannah's lower back to guide her forward and watch the pedestrians milling about the sidewalks. Kee takes point as James drives off.

I wouldn't say I like their security structure. There should always be at least two security personnel with Hannah.

Kee opens the townhouse's front door, and we all step into the entryway, "Wait here while I check the house." I know she's saying it for my benefit because Hannah likely goes through this daily.

I keep my hands to myself, fighting the instinct to comfort her.

James walks in the front door as Kee returns to the entryway. "Okay, the house is clear. You can come in."

Hannah doesn't look at me as she slides past Kee into the house. "James, could you please grab the medkit from the upstairs bathroom?"

"On it," he says, heading towards the staircase.

I walk into the house. It's bright, clean, and minimal. There aren't any photos on the walls, no personal touches. She's got all the essentials you need to furnish a home, but it doesn't seem to be "lived" in.

Is this a safe house?

Hannah stops halfway down the hallway and turns to me. "Join me in the sunroom?"

I follow her down the hall, taking in the house's bareness as we walk past the kitchen and living room to the back. Opening the door to what I think will be an outdoor porch, I'm stunned as we step out into an enclosed sunroom.

This is the room that she spends the most time in. It's almost too bright. Three walls are made of glass, and there are so many house plants of various types that it feels like I'm standing outside.

A light blue to gray ombre rug covers the floor, and the furniture consists of a small table with two chairs, a hanging egg chair, and a small comfy chair in the far corner. This is Hannah's sanctuary.

I must have been standing there with my mouth hanging open. "I'm guessing you like the sunroom?" she says with a lilt of laughter.

"It's…bright," I say, looking at her.

She smiles, but her smile doesn't reach her eyes.

"Take off your jacket and shirt."

I snap around to look at her again. "What?"

"Your ribs? I want to take a look at them, remember?"

"Oh, right. Sorry, I forgot." I look around; Kee and James are nowhere in sight, and apparently, James has already dropped off the medkit. He must have snuck it in while I looked around like a dumbass.

She's sitting at the table for two, with the medkit on the table, looking at me expectantly. Her demeanor has completely changed now that we are in the house. She was so scared and uncertain when we were outside, but here, in her space, she is confident. I can almost feel it coming off her in waves. She raises her eyebrows at me and gestures to her seat.

I take my jacket off and toss it over the back of the chair but leave the t-shirt.

"Now, you're modest?" she asks sarcastically.

"I don't usually take my shirt off right away when getting to know someone."

"I doubt that."

"I think you have a preconceived notion of who I am, Doctor." I'm leaning forward with my hands clasped, making too much eye contact.

She shifts in her chair, and there it is. Her skin flushes under my gaze, and I watch it climb up her neck to her cheeks, staining them a soft pink. She shifts again and clears her throat, reaching to tuck her hair behind her ear.

Fuck she's cute when she's nervous.

I clasp my hands tighter to avoid reaching out to tuck an errant strand of strawberry blonde hair behind her ear.

Now that I've got her off-balance, I pull my shirt over my head.

"Oh!" She tries to stifle her surprise, but I expect it and take no offense. It's the reaction I always get when someone sees me without my shirt on for the first time.

Having removed my shirt, I put it over the back of my chair before turning to meet her gaze. Her eyes are glued to my chest, my scars, and the area where I should have breasts, but instead, I have a flat chest. I wait for the questions and give her time to understand what she's seeing.

She immediately looks up. "Sorry, I don't mean to stare. I wasn't expecting to see…that you…" She trails off, the red in her cheeks darkening.

"What are your preferred pronouns?" I can't help but smile at her for asking.

"She/They. I'm genderfluid and had top surgery almost a decade ago." It's taken me almost as long to be able to say that sentence out loud with any sense of confidence. I continue, "I'm biologically a woman, but there are times where I identify more as a male than female and other times where I'm somewhere in the middle. What about you? Your preferred pronouns?"

I sit back, feeling a weight lift off my shoulders, having shown her and gotten it out of the way.

"She/Her," she says softly. I can see the wheels turning in her head as she runs her eyes down my body. Not only my chest but also the fact that tattoos cover a large portion of my chest. I know it will take her a moment to compute everything.

"It's a lot to take in," I say, trying to ease the uncomfortable silence that has fallen over the sunroom.

She smiles and points to the dark bruise on my ribcage, "Can you move closer so I can better look at your ribs?"

I slide my chair closer.

CHAPTER 18

Hannah

As Gray slides her chair closer, I know I shouldn't stare at her chest, but I wasn't expecting to see a bare chest. I'm sure that Gray saw the shock on my face.

What Gray doesn't know is that it's more than shock. I'm overwhelmed with what I feel for her, which surprises me more than how Gray looks.

I want to reach out. I want to run my hands down Gray's chest and stomach. I want to touch her everywhere and for Gray to feel me. I've never felt this way for someone so quickly. Felt this attraction and pull that I can't seem to explain.

When we first met in the club, I told myself it was just lust, but I'm not sure if that's all. Something about Gray calls to me draws me in, and the longer I'm around her, the farther I sink. I know I need to pull back, but I'm unsure if I'll be able to.

Gray sits up straighter as I reach my hand out to examine her ribs. Gray's skin is soft, even though it looks like it should be rough with scars, bruises, and tattoos. Everything about Gray screams to stay away. Yet, there is a softness to her that I can't explain.

When I look at Gray, though, I see a different story. Gray's sadness and loneliness blanket her, yet I've seen flashes of kindness and a playful side at the club.

Gray's duality is what draws me in.

I know I should listen to my instincts and keep my distance.

"How did you get this bruise?" I ask, sliding my hand over the bruised ribs, which are already turning various shades of blue and black. Gray's stomach twitches and tightens under my hands, reacting to my touch.

The skin around the bruise is turning dark red and purple with swelling. Gray must be in a lot of pain, but she hides it well.

Gray clears her throat and shifts under my hand. "I think it was a punch or kick. I'm not entirely sure, though."

I look up at them, trying to hide the concern and shock that runs through me.

"You were punched or kicked, and you don't remember which? Did you hit your head too?"

Gray looks at me sheepishly, scoffing and scratching the back of her head. "Well, I think I did. I've got a bit of a lump."

"I'll take a look at that next," I say as I gently examine the bruises on Gray's ribs.

"You should go to the hospital and get an x-ray to ensure you didn't fracture or break a rib."

"Mmhm, not a fan of hospitals," Gray says softly, her breath brushing the top of my forehead. "I'm pretty sure they're just bruised. Nothing feels broken."

"You know what broken ribs feel like?" I ask, although I already know the answer.

Gray doesn't respond immediately, prompting me to look up. My breath seems to stutter and then stop in my chest. My face is only a few inches from hers. So close, I can see every freckle on Gray's olive-skinned face. So close.

My eyes drift to Gray's lips on their own, and suddenly my free hand is on her other side, holding onto Gray. I can't seem to control my body.

Neither of us moves or says anything. Gray's heart beats in her neck as our breath mingles in the space between us. I can't tear my eyes away from her lips. The urge to kiss is overwhelming. Gray has full dark red, swollen lips, swollen from the cut and bruises. Yet, as I gaze at her split lip, I imagine this is what they would look like after being kissed.

I want to kiss them.

My hand, acting on its own again, gently cups her face. I run my thumb over the split in her lip and the rest of her bottom lip. The tip of Gray's tongue glides over her split lip, tracing the path of my finger.

My entire body tightens.

Gray swallows, shifting in the chair and pulling back from my hands.

"Sorry," Gray says, clearing her throat and avoiding my eyes.

The heat starts crawling up my neck to my cheeks as Gray pulls away, sitting back. I immediately miss the feel of her skin, the softness, and the warmth. I'm unsure what to say, making the moment even more awkward as we look at each other.

I clear my throat and stand up, deciding that ignoring what just happened is the best way to go.

"Let's take a look at your head." I try to inject some light into my voice. I'm desperate to ease the tension and awkwardness.

Gray doesn't respond as I move behind her chair.

CHAPTER 19

Gray

Hannah quickly stands up, moving behind me. I'm still trying to steady myself and figure out what just happened. I can feel the warmth of her hands on my face, the fire left behind by her thumb on my lip. The look on her face as she followed the movement of my tongue as it chased her thumb. Her pupils dilate, her breathing quickens, and the pink flush creeps up her neck when nervous or flustered. It's seared in my mind.

Hannah's hands move through my hair, starting at the front of my head and moving back until she finds the bump on the back of my head. As her long delicate fingers move through my hair, the urge to lean back into her is almost too much to ignore. It's soothing in a way I haven't experienced before. It's comforting, it's unfamiliar, and it's lovely.

I jump at the pain and surprise as she presses the area around the bump. The pain breaks me from the grasp of comfort and tosses me back into the harsh light of reality.

"Sorry," her voice barely whispers. "You definitely have a good-sized bump here. Did you lose consciousness at all?"

"No, I didn't."

"Are you nauseous? Any headaches?" She's in full doctor mode as she feels around the wound before walking around to face me.

"No, nothing's been out of the ordinary."

"Well, you probably have a concussion, and your ribs are bruised." She's twisting her hands in her lap while talking and looking anywhere but at me.

"I can give you some of the usual meds to help with the pain and swelling if you want them."

"That's alright. I've already taken some today and have my own meds at home. I'll be sure to watch for any other symptoms."

Hannah nods, still avoiding me.

"Thanks for checking me out, though." I reach cautiously, ready for rejection, and place my hand over hers, hoping to steady her.

Hannah looks up at me from behind her lashes, a light pink dusting her cheeks. Her green eyes find mine before drifting to look at my lips.

"Can I apply a new liquid bandage?"

"Wha. Oh, ha yeah, that'd be great, thanks." The words stick in my throat as my pulse ratchets up. I swallow hard as she slides her chair closer, positioning her legs on either side of mine. I try to steady my breathing but can't control my body when she's this close to me. Hannah gently applies the bandage, adding several steri-strips to secure the cut until the glue fully sets.

"There. Don't get punched the next couple of days again, okay?" She smiles, drawing her hands away from my face, her fingertips lingering for just a second on my jaw, her eyes lingering on my lips.

Hannah leans forward slightly, our eyes meeting, breathing mingling as we both try to resist. The urge to kiss her is overwhelming, and I lean in, unaware of my movements. My body seems to be acting on its own again.

I take in everything: her red lips, pink cheeks, and red hair make her green eyes and freckles pop. She's beautiful.

"No, kissing..."

"What?"

"No, kissing. Your lip." We're still inches apart as she whispers each breathless word.

Neither of us moves from where we are. Her hands are on my face, mine on her legs.

I clear my throat, blinking rapidly. "Right, no kissing." A flutter runs through my body, "I…would like to kiss you soon, though, if that's okay."

Hannah nods slowly, her eyes fluttering as she glances from my eyes to my lips.

"Yes, I would like that very much."

Smiling like a fool, I lean back in my chair, breaking the spell. Reaching over my shoulder, I grab my shirt. I can feel her watching my every move and can't help but feel self-conscious yet satisfied as she studies my body.

"Shall we check in with Kee and James? I want to learn more about what's happening, if you don't mind."

Her demeanor changes immediately from blushing and flustered to nervous and pale.

Hannah stands up quickly and pushes her chair back under the table, gathering her medical supplies without responding. Sighing, she stops, dropping everything back to the table, and turns to face me.

"It's complicated, messy, and scary, and I hate thinking about it, and…I don't want to scare you away. I like you, and we just met and…"

"It's okay. I know it's scary, but if I know what's going on, I think it will help me better understand the situation. I also want to learn more about you, about everything. You only need to share as much or as little as you want. I won't pressure you to tell me about it if it makes you uncomfortable."

Hannah nods, tucking a loose strand of hair behind her right ear. "Let's go talk to Kee and James, then."

I follow her from the sunroom's warmth into the drab den's interior.

CHAPTER 20

Hannah

'm still wrapping my head around everything I saw and felt as Gray and I walk through the house. My heart is thundering in my ears as I struggle to control my breathing. I would have gone in for the kiss if Gray hadn't pulled away, even though I said no to kissing. I would have done it. I should have.

Why am I so scared of everything?

Everything about Gray draws me to her. The color of her eyes, her lips, the rasp in her voice. Gray makes me yearn.

I'm getting flush again, I can feel it creeping up my neck, and I try to focus on anything other than the imposing figure walking quietly beside me.

"Are you alright?" Gray asks softly.

Ugh, she must have noticed.

I can't seem to form words around the lump in my throat, so I simply nod and offer a weak smile.

Kee and James are both in the front room, James at the front window and Kee at the table in the far corner of the bare dark room.

Looking up, Kee gives us both a nod and a knowing smile. James, a quick nod in our general direction, lets us know that he heard us come in.

"Gray would like to know more about my situation from a safety perspective. Could one of you fill her in, please?"

My voice shakes, and my stomach turns even though I'm trying to sound and act strong. My palms grow sweaty, and a shake rolls through my body. I can feel the edge of panic until Gray places a hand on the small of my back.

"Take a breath," she whispers. I can't bring myself to look at her, as the shame is too much. I'm so weak. Gray's gaze is like a fire that moves over me as she watches me to ensure I'm okay.

Nodding, I draw in a breath that catches at the back of my throat on the sob threatening to come out. I take another, focusing only on the feel of Gray's hand pressing into my back.

"Better?"

I nod. Exchanging glances Kee and James settle into the chairs across from the sofa.

We sit side-by-side across from James and Kee. They look as uncomfortable as I feel.

"You're sure about this, Hannah?" Kee asks.

Knotting and unknotting my fingers in my lap, I nod again.

"Hannah's father is District Attorney Marshal Winters." Gray stiffens next to me upon hearing his name.

Does she know him? Is it normal for a bouncer to know the name of an acting D.A.?

Nodding, Gray gestures for James to continue.

"As you know, it's common for a D.A. to try a variety of cases, and sometimes people don't like that. In Mr. Winters' case, the individual being investigated found out and has been threatening Mr. Winters and his family. There have been threats and physical attacks on Hannah and her father, so Kee and I are here."

Gray goes still.

"After the first attack, Hannah's father started taking the threats more seriously. Since then, there have been multiple attacks on Hannah. They have stopped since we moved to this new location and have added security besides just the two of us."

Gray continues to nod beside me, taking it all in. I imagine this is the point in the conversation where she will get up to leave. After hearing all this, I can't imagine what is going through an outsider's mind. This is too much for even me to handle, and it's my life.

But Gray is just sitting there listening as James lays it all out. She doesn't look shocked or scared. Gray seems to be taking it all in, and I can see that this is something that she's used to.

"I'm sure you have questions," I say as James pauses.

"Well, I'm glad you're okay, and the attacks have been unsuccessful. It's good that Kee and James are here, and it's good to hear that more security personnel are in place. I have a few recommendations, but I'll save those for a different conversation with Kee and James."

James shakes his head, and Gray continues before he can say anything.

"What else is being done to stop the attacks and threats?"

Kee stands, "Well, the authorities are involved as much as possible, but the main focus is getting Mr. Winters' investigation wrapped up as soon as possible. He will walk if we pursue legal action based on what we know and the evidence that we currently have. We don't have much tying him to the attacks, so there's not much we can do that won't impact the D.A.'s investigation."

"So…you're just sitting and waiting for her father to close the case? It sounds like you're playing with fire. Isn't that, I don't know, a bit dangerous? Also, who exactly is this person that is being investigated?"

"Listen, we're doing everything we can, but we have to work within the system. Which is something you probably don't know about. I can't give you any information on who is being investigated."

"Sounds like some bullshit." Gray's voice is dark, low, and angry.

James stands next to Kee now. "You got any more questions or are you just going to sit there and bitch."

Gray's left eyebrow arches up as she eyes Kee and James; Gray shakes her head with a smirk while placing a reassuring hand on my thigh. "I'll let you know if anything else comes to mind."

Gray faces me. "Let me know what I can do to make you feel safer when I'm around."

I know Gray is saying this to make me feel better, but I already have a team of bodyguards. I don't need, nor do I want, a third. I want Gray to be something more than safety. I don't need to be babied. I don't need to be pampered. I need someone to want, yearn for, and desire me.

I force a smile to my face and nod, leaning into Gray's solid shoulder.

I'll bring it up later when Kee and James aren't around.

CHAPTER 21

Gray

Sitting on the couch with Hannah seems normal, as if we weren't just talking about how some crime boss attacked her and her family. I need to know more. Marshal Winters is a name I know well, which makes me concerned. If her dad is caught up in what I think he is, this will get really complicated and won't end well for us.

I try to push it all to the back of my mind so I can sit in the moment and enjoy that Hannah doesn't appear to be scared of me, and if anything, it feels like this has brought us closer together. I hope to keep her safe and give her what she needs to feel comfortable and safe with me.

Settling back onto the couch, Hannah winds her arm through mine, hugging me into her body as she curls her legs up and snuggles into my side. I can't help but stiffen. This is unfamiliar, the feelings of warmth. I don't know the last time someone cuddled with me. My surprise must have shown on my face as Kee chuckles softly from across the room.

She and James both get up, leaving the room so we can get comfortable and relax.

I know I'm rigid, which can't be comfortable for her, so I try to relax on the couch, but I don't know what to do with my hands or body. After sitting there awkwardly for a few minutes, I settle into her. Putting a hand on her leg and resting my head atop hers.

We fit well together.

It feels natural now that I've given in to it. Whatever it is. I suppose this is what ordinary people do when they like one another. The only relationship I've been in recently was toxic and ended badly. I've been using my work as a shield lately when in reality, I've been excruciatingly lonely.

I can't help how I feel for Hannah, even though I know we likely won't last. I typically would end things before they could even begin, but this time I want to see how far it goes. Maybe it's real. Perhaps this is what I need, even though it will be messy.

"You're not going to run now, are you?" Hannah's voice is a soft caress in the dim room.

"I'm not running. I don't plan to."

She tightens her hold on my arm, snuggling closer. Within minutes her breathing evens, and she's fallen asleep with her head on my shoulder.

I'm definitely not running now. I can feel myself drifting and struggling to keep my eyes open as Hannah's soft breathing lulls me to sleep. I settle in, putting my feet on the coffee table and leaning into her.

CHAPTER 22

Hannah

'm warm and comfortable. The smell of sandalwood and cocoa butter is light and just tickles my senses as I pull in deep breaths trying to coax myself back to sleep. Sometime during my nap, I've gone from Gray's shoulder to her lap. I'm surprised she hasn't moved yet.

I'm unsure how long I've been asleep, but it's been at least an hour or two. I should get up, but I'm so comfortable and calm now that getting up is the last thing I want to do.

Gray's leg muscle tightens, then relaxes under my head. Her legs must be stiff. I open my eyes slowly and see Gray's legs propped on the coffee table, her arm runs parallel to my side, and Gray's hand gently rests on my hip. This seems normal like my world isn't being torn apart by a psychopath crime lord like someone hasn't been trying to kill me.

How is this happening, and why is it happening now?

I haven't actively been trying to date or find someone, and Gray shows up now that my life is falling apart. I'm worried that Gray will change her mind and start running or that this will be too much and will ruin whatever we are beginning. It seems too good to be true.

My relaxed state is officially ruined as I ponder everything going on. Inhaling deeply, I sit up, stretching my arms above my head. As I move and start stretching, I look over at Gray and can't help but laugh.

"What? What's so funny?" she asks, looking at me with sleepy eyes.

"Your hair is…it's…" I can't stop laughing as I look at her short hair that seems to be pointing in every direction.

"Is it bad?" Gray's voice is husky, and I laugh even harder.

Reaching out, I pat it down, taming it as Gray sits, looking at me with soft eyes and a small smile. It's a genuine smile that reaches her eyes and wrinkles the corners. I stop patting Gray's hair and let my hand caress through it along the side of her face. Gray closes her eyes and leans into my hand, turning her face slightly to kiss my palm.

I can't seem to make myself move, to take my hand away. I don't want to break the spell. I want to stay here for as long as possible. I take in every inch of Gray's face, from the bruises and cuts to the crow's feet by her eyes and the slight dusting of freckles across the bridge of her nose and cheeks.

No kissing, Hannah, that's what you said.

I lean forward and lightly place my lips on the corner of Gray's mouth, away from the split. I move from her mouth to kiss her bruised cheek softly before moving to the cut above her eyebrow. Gray's breath quickens as I map out her face with my kisses. Gray's breath tickles my throat as it mingles with my loose hair. I continue kissing the aches and pains on Gray's face and hear her audibly swallow before her hands find my hips, gripping them lightly as I continue to peruse her face with my kisses.

I want more.

My lips find their way back to Gray's, and I kiss both sides avoiding the split yet desperately wanting to ignore my advice and kiss her harder. I want to kiss Gray with every fiber of my being.

"Ummm, sorry to interrupt," Kee's voice cuts through the fog that has consumed my brain, and I jerk away, accidentally hitting Gray's ribs. A hiss escapes her mouth as she touches her ribs lightly and glances down.

"Oh my God, I'm sorry, Kee surprised me!" I want to reach out and take the pain away, but there isn't anything I can do to make this pain go away.

"It's okay." Gray smiles, and I look at Kee, shooting her the dirtiest look I can manage.

"Hate to break this up, kiddos, but we have a schedule to keep." That's all she says before turning and walking out of the room.

"What schedule?" Gray asks.

"It's nothing. It's more for Kee and James than for me. They have a schedule and expect me to stay on it with them."

"Okay, Thank you for the walk, the medical care, and the kisses. I had a wonderful time." Gray's lopsided smile tightens my stomach, and I fight the urge to kiss her again.

Blinking rapidly before my body acts of its own accord, I disengage and stand up from the couch.

"I'll call or text you?" Suddenly, I'm shy and embarrassed. "If that's all right."

"Anytime," Gray says, reaching back for my hand as she heads towards the door. Kee is in the kitchen, and James is nowhere to be seen, so he's probably on car duty and sitting outside.

"Bye." Gray leans in, and at first, I think she's going to kiss me on the lips, but Gray tilts her chin up and kisses me on the forehead instead. A soft, delicate graze across my forehead leaves me lightheaded and wanting.

Gray opens the door and walks out onto the street with a wave, giving James a wave as she passes by the car.

I can't breathe. My heart is beating so fast that I feel like I might die.

Holy shit.

CHAPTER 23

Gray

"Holy shit!" Marcus shouts, giving me a rough slap on the shoulder. "So you and the doc had a make out sesh!" He's got the biggest shit-eating grin, and I know he will never stop bringing it up. I should not have told him.

"Don't call it that. Who even says that anymore?" We're hanging out at the bar before the club opens. Typically, I wouldn't have said anything to him. Still, I must have a look on my face because he knew something had happened immediately.

"Well, I'll be damned. I haven't seen or heard of you being around someone like this. Are you sure it's a good idea? The doc doesn't seem like your type of lady."

"Marcus, the less you say, the better." Grabbing a bottle of water from Phil, our new barback, I retreat to the far-right corner of the club and try to mentally prepare myself for the night. I'm just settling into the darkness when my earpiece screeches to life.

"Don't forget, the boss is here tonight. I heard a rumor that Kiera is with him, so you might want to stick to the shadows as much as possible."

Fuck me. Of course, Kiera would be here tonight.

She's trouble, always has been, and always will be. Just hearing her name makes my skin crawl and my stomach tense, but not in a good way. In our game of cat and mouse, she's the hunter, and I'm the prey.

No matter how often I resist and say no, she constantly pushes the boundaries between us, and her dad, my boss, doesn't help. Dimitri likes to assign me to act as Kiera's bodyguard while she's in town, and I swear he does it just so he can watch me squirm.

"I will definitely stick to the shadows tonight," I say as I sink further into the darkness around me. Tonight the dark places of Midnight and I are going to be one.

"Good call," Marcus responds, and I see him throw me a thumbs up from his position on the second-floor landing.

Idiot.

Turning, I come face to face with the one person I don't want to see tonight.

"Kiera!" I instinctively take a step back, putting some distance between us.

"Gray, how have you been?" Reaching up, she runs a red-nailed finger down the scar on the left side of my face.

I try not to cringe as I remember how I got the scar. To how she knelt over me, and Dimitri's men held me down so that she could mark me.

I swallow and take another step back, out of her reach.

"I didn't realize you were going to be in town."

Her smile reminds me of the Cheshire Cat's, all gleaming white teeth paired with cold dead eyes.

"Have you missed me?" She moves forward, touching my chest and leaning forward until her face is a few inches from mine.

Kiera is much shorter than I am, but we're eye-to-eye in her six-inch heels. Tonight she's in a skin-tight, black leather dress that hugs every curve of her voluptuous body. Her black hair is cut in a severe long bob with straight bangs that bleed into her black eyebrows. Her pale skin is highlighted by the brightness of her red lips and nails. Everything about Kiera screams danger. I never should have gotten involved with her, but there's a part of me that's drawn to the threat or a part that was attracted to it.

Now, I can barely look at her without feeling a knot in my stomach and panic settling into my chest.

"Nothing to say for yourself? We haven't seen each other for months."

"I don't have anything to say to you, Kiera."

Smiling, she leans in again, her red claws digging into my suit-clad chest. "I'll ask Father if you can accompany me during my time in town."

My breath stutters, and I feel a cold shiver down my spine.

"I'd rather not," I say quietly, trying to stand my ground and not show that I'm actually terrified of her.

"Don't be too bold, Gray. You'll regret it." The words slither from her pursed red lips, and my heart feels like it's going to burst from the pressure of holding my breath.

"Actually, I don't think I need Father's permission. Why don't you and I go grab something to eat right now? Just a snack."

I want to say no, but everything in my body tells me to go along. I can't go through what I did before with my face. I can't do that again. I won't make it this time. I'll break.

Swallowing my fear and panic, I nod.

Kiera slides her arm through mine and leads me towards the club's front doors. I glance back at Marcus. The concern on his face does nothing to make me feel better.

"Don't worry, I'll have you back before the club opens. Father won't even know you're not around."

Luke gives me a concerned look as we reach the door, and I'm tempted to ask him for help, to ask anyone for help. But Kiera is one person I can't escape. I despise her, yet I need to be around her and be in her good favor.

I give Luke a nod and a quick smile to let him know everything is good, and I walk out of Midnight with Kiera.

A line forms at the door, and heads turn as we walk out. They're all looking at Kiera. She has that effect on people. The men want her, and the women want to be her.

Grinning, she struts down the line until we reach the corner where her favorite food spot is. Kiera says they make the best Bird's Milk Cake or Ptichye Moloko.

"Do you want a piece, love?" Kiera acts as if nothing has ever happened between us. As if she didn't carve a line down my face.

"I'm good."

"You need to lighten up, Gray. You're no fun when you're like this. Remember how much fun we used to have when we were together?" She runs a nail through the middle of the slice of cake, bringing it to her lips and licking the cake from her finger. She then reaches over, grabs me by the back of my neck, and pulls me in until our lips touch.

I'm trying to pull my head back, but her grip is firm, and she's surprised me with the move.

Kiera's tongue snakes out between her lips and flicks across mine as I turn my face away.

Huffing, she pushes me back, her nails leaving a trail on the back of my neck.

"Take me back to the club."

Turning away from her, I glance across the street and make eye contact with someone getting out of a black sedan across the street.

Fuck. It's James.

He doesn't break eye contact as I keep walking arm-in-arm with Kiera to the club doors. He also doesn't move away from the vehicle.

Is Hannah in there?

Did she see us?

CHAPTER 24

Hannah

"Will we be going to Midnight?"

"No, I don't think so, Kee. Not tonight. I'm exhausted from the week and am on call tomorrow morning. I'd like to relax and decompress tonight."

"Bummer," Kee mutters as she walks back to her station in the kitchen. She seems more disappointed than me. I think she has a thing for the older bouncer, Marcus. She's mentioned him several times since our last visit to Midnight. Yeah, there's definitely something there. I did not peg Marcus as Kee's type, but perhaps I don't know Kee as well as I think I do. He seems to have a sense of humor that is very much like Kee's, so maybe that's what attracts her to him.

A heavy sigh escapes as I settle into the sunroom, ready for a relaxing night.

I've been debating going to Midnight's since the first time and my walk with Gray, but I want to take things slow, and showing up at Gray's place of work doesn't feel slow to me.

Hey, I'm heading to Midnight's tonight. They have a special DJ playing, and I've been dying to see him. Do you want to come along?

You've got to be kidding me!

"Do you and Cassie have a text going or something?" I ask, looking at Kee.

"No, why?"

"Cassie wants to go to Midnight's tonight and asked if I want to join."

"Are you going to go?"

"I can't very well let Cassie go by herself. God only knows what kind of trouble she'll get herself into."

"That's my girl! I'll let James and the team know, and we'll prepare. Just let us know when you want to go."

I'll meet you there. Don't do anything too crazy in the meantime!

Walking out to the car, the brisk air momentarily brings me back to myself. I can't believe I'm going to the club again. What has gotten into me!

Kee and James are in the front, neither chatting as they watch the people and vehicles around us.

From the window, I watch as we move from the old cobbled alleys and family homes of Olde Town to the abandoned industrial area where Club Midnight and a handful of other businesses can be found.

"Did you see that?" I hear Kee mutter from the front, and I turn to look out the front window, but whatever they saw has already passed.

"You take her in, and I'll park the car. Don't mention it." James says.

What are they talking about?

James pulls up to the front of the club, and Kee jumps out, opening the door and helping me out.

Luke recognizes me and lets Kee and I cut the line, and before I know it, I'm walking into Club Midnight again.

It's been two weeks since the last time I was here. Since the night we met, since our walk.

Walking in, I head straight for the bar, hoping to find Cassie. I don't look around. I'm only focused on getting to the bar and getting something to ease my nerves.

I can do this. It will be fine.

CHAPTER 25

Gray

Her movement's smoothness catches my eye as she weaves around the pulsing bodies.

Holy shit, she came back.

I haven't heard from or seen Hannah in at least two weeks. I was beginning to wonder if I would hear from her again.

I still can't take my eyes off her as she heads to the same spot at the bar as the night we met.

Don't get distracted, Gray. Focus on your job, and don't get sidetracked.

Dimitri and Kiera are both here tonight, and the last thing I need is for them to see me unfocused and distracted by a pretty clubgoer.

She's more than that, though. Ugh, what am I even thinking! I don't even know her!

Get. It. Together.

I shake my head and straighten my tie as I focus on the crush of bodies on the dancefloor. The club is packed, the DJ is winding them up, and it's only a matter of time before they combust. Who knows how long it will last? Everything seems to be fine in Midnight for the time being.

I fight the urge to look for Hannah at the back bar. I know she's there with Kee and James on either side. Even telling myself not to look can't stop me. My eyes are drawn to Hannah. She's clutching her white wine and is watching the dancefloor. I can see how tense she is from my spot on the second-floor landing and know it's because she's actively trying not to look in my direction.

I'm making her feel this way. I make her uncomfortable.

Shame washes over me. I never should have given her my number. I was way out of line. I would have ruined her life. It's for the best.

I'll steer clear of her tonight. I don't want to make her any more uncomfortable than she already is.

CHAPTER 26

Hannah

"Hey, isn't that Gray?" Cassie's voice is so loud I swear everyone in Midnight can hear it.

"Cassie, Jesus. Could you be more obvious?" I'm horrified by what she's doing. She's actually waving at Gray, standing on the second-floor balcony.

Gray doesn't wave back. She doesn't make any indication that she sees Cassie waving.

I feel like I'm back in high school. I'm back to being the awkward teen with no idea who she is or what she wants, terrified, embarrassed, and ashamed.

"I think we should leave Gray alone tonight. She is working, after all," James says. Something in his voice makes me turn to look at him. He sounds pissed, and I'm not sure why.

"Are you okay?" I say, leaning towards him so I don't have to fight to be heard over the music.

"I don't think you should worry about that one anymore. Gray isn't a good person," James says.

"James! What has gotten into you? You don't even know her!"

"I know more than you think, and I don't think you should pursue anything with Gray. Especially not now."

I roll my eyes at James and turn to commiserate with Kee.

"James is right. It would be best if you stayed away from Gray for now. She's no good for you."

"What the hell is going on with you two?" I glance between Kee and James, entirely at a loss.

"Well, I think she can do whatever the fuck she wants to!" Cassie shouts, leaning over the bar and ordering two shots of vodka.

Passing one to me, I hold my breath and take it to prove a point to Kee and James.

I almost throw up.

I take a sip of my wine quickly to try to chase the taste of the vodka away. It doesn't do much to help, and I can feel the vodka slinking its way through my body.

Tonight is going to be fun.

CHAPTER 27

Gray

'm not sure if tonight could get any worse. Knowing that both Kiera and Hannah are here makes me anxious. I have to ignore Hannah the entire night. If I don't and Kiera sees, that could cause trouble. I hate to think about what she might do if she gets jealous.

Hannah has enough that she's dealing with. Adding a crazy possessive ex to the mix won't do anyone any favors.

I want to approach Hannah and tell her how I've missed her over the last few weeks. I would call but thought better of it and didn't want to cause her any additional trouble. I have so many things I want to say to her, but I can't. I need to distance myself from her, and that's never been more critical than tonight.

"Gray, did you see Hannah come in?" Luke's voice echoes in my ear. Great, everyone must know what happened between us.

"I did, Luke. Thank you for letting me know." I hope he gets the hint from the dryness of my tone that he needs to back off and keep his nose out of my business.

"Just wanted to make sure you didn't miss her, not like you could anyway."

"Okay, Luke! I get the hint; please stay off the comms with this shit."

I look to the bar out of the corner of my eye and catch a glimpse of Hannah talking casually to Kee and James. She seems to have loosened up some, and maybe, just maybe, she's enjoying herself. Her friend Cassie has already disappeared into the sea of bodies below me.

Every fiber of my being wants to go to Hannah, needs to go to her. I want to tell her I've been thinking about her, but tonight is not the night to do this.

"Gray, you're up to roam. I'm coming to switch out with you." Marcus has been oddly quiet tonight. Maybe he gets the situation and understands that sometimes it's better to let someone go than to cling to them when you know all you'll do is hurt them.

"Copy, rotating now," I reply, moving down the steps and walking towards the bar, towards Hannah.

I hope to walk by her without confrontation or awkward moments between us.

I have no such luck.

As I start walking past the bar, someone on the dancefloor lurches forward, bumping me and sending me right into Kee as she stands beside Hannah.

"What the fu… Marcus, you're fucking dead," I whisper venomously. I trail off as I see who pushed me.

Smirking, he shrugs and almost skips off to his next station.

"Sorry about that," I mutter, scowling after him.

"It's no trouble," a slightly drunk Hannah smiles at me, giggling as she sways to the music.

"You're drunk."

"Nope, just tipsy. Come dance with me!" She grabs my hand before I can protest and leads me towards the dancefloor.

"Hannah, wait, I can't. I'm…I'm working!" No matter how I protest, she pulls me towards the dancefloor.

"Hannah! Stop, please." Finally, she stops, but we are in the middle of the dancefloor. Surrounded by the gyrating bodies of everyone around us.

Throwing her hands over my neck, she starts swaying to the rhythm, and even though I'm trying hard not to move with her, it's as if instinct takes over, and soon my hands are on her hips, and I'm swaying in time with her.

The music is pounding, but Hannah seems to find a slower rhythm that still works with the beat of the music. I lose myself in her movement and forget where I am and what I'm supposed to be doing.

A dangerous thing to do in a place like Midnight.

CHAPTER 28

Hannah

It will be less awkward if I act like I'm a bit drunker than I am. It'll make me bold and help me do what I want, what I'm too scared to do. If I make an idiot of myself, I'll just claim that I was drunk, and if Gray rejects me, I'll just play it off and act like it doesn't matter.

That was the plan until Marcus helped me by bumping into Gray so hard that she stumbled into us. I took that as my sign and grabbed her hand before she could return to walking her route. I would have to thank him later for giving me a hand.

Be bold, Hannah. Just be bold.

I ignore Gray as she protests, knowing this will get her in trouble, but I don't care. I want to dance, I want to spend time with her, I want to be close to her. I want all these things, and I'm only brave enough to do it if I pretend to be drunker than I actually am, so I stop second-guessing myself.

I start to sway to the EDM beat that's playing through the club. The underlying melody is perfect for slower dancing. I connect with it instantly, dragging Gray into the melody with me.

My arms are around her neck, my head on her shoulder, and her hands, although hesitantly, are around my waist and then my body, pulling me closer until there isn't any space between us. We become one as we let the music take over.

It's beautiful not to think about anything and focus on the music and how my body moves. I lose myself to the rhythm and forget that Gray is there with me as her hands slide from my waist, untethering me to the world. I let loose. I haven't felt this free in months, maybe even years.

Except I want to focus on one other thing, Gray. I want her to join me in the freedom. I reach for her hands, open my eyes, and pull her close again. Embracing her and throwing my arms around her neck, I feel the laughter bubbling inside me and letting it burst free. I shake my head, giggling, and let Gray spin me around the dancefloor.

This is what happiness is. This is what it feels like to be happy. This feels right; I want to stay like this.

I look at Gray and can't help myself. I kiss her hard and without care. I can tell I shock her because kissing me back takes her a few seconds, but I think my soul leaves my body when she does.

She's controlled in her kissing, letting me take the lead, holding back yet giving me everything I'm asking for. We are lost in the moment until Gray jerks her head back, hand reaching for her earpiece.

CHAPTER 29

Gray

I let the movement of her body and the music draw me in and make me forget where I am and what I'm supposed to be doing. I also forget that eyes and ears are everywhere, even when lost on the dancefloor and surrounded by drunken dancers.

I lose myself in the moment and let Hannah take the lead. I'm giving her the reins to do as she wants. Right now, she wants to move with the melody of the music, and I'm perfectly okay with that.

I can feel her heart beating against my chest, and I try to sink into her as much as possible, pulling her closer until the space between us doesn't exist. Her hands around my neck begin to move. One stays around my neck while the other works its way up my back into my hair, which lasts for a moment before moving down again and resting on my shoulder.

She wants to move more with the music but hesitates to let loose.

I step back from her and let her move more freely to the music, watching as she starts to bounce and jump around with the beat of the dance music. I'm not watching anything else or anyone else around us. All I can see is the pure joy on her face as she lets the music take over.

She almost looks like a different person. The tension lines

typically around her eyes and mouth are gone. She seemed relaxed and entirely in her body for the first time since I met her.

This is who Hannah is, she's joy and happiness, and someone has taken that away from her.

I stop moving to the music and watch her. I want desperately to kiss her but don't want to drop her out of the music. I want her to stay there, in that sweet spot, for as long as possible.

Her eyes closed, moving and jumping to the music, not caring about who sees it or what she looks like. Nothing but joy and wild abandon.

"Gray, you need to get back to your post ASAP!" Marcus' voice seems distant, and in my lusty haze, I barely hear him.

"Gray! Your post. Now! Kiera saw you and Hannah!" Those last words make my stomach turn, and I jerk away from Hannah, pushing my earpiece in so I can hear Marcus more clearly.

"Repeat."

"You heard me, Kiera saw you and Hannah, and she's on her way up to Dimitri's office right now."

Fuck.

"I have to go back to work." It pains me to leave her in more than one way, but I'm in deep shit, and it won't be pretty if I don't get my shit together soon.

Hannah nods, seemingly in a daze. I take her hand and lead her off the dancefloor and back to James and Kee, still at the bar. Both of them scowling in my direction.

"I'll try to find you again before you leave, but don't wait for me." The truth is that I don't want to give Kiera a chance to "bump" into Hannah. There's no telling what she would do. "It's probably best to leave before it gets crazy here."

I give Hannah a smile and start walking my route. Looking over my shoulder, I see Dimitri and Kiera standing on the top level, looking down at me.

This won't be good.

CHAPTER 30

Hannah

Following Gray's eyes, I look up at the club's top floor, where the offices are, and see a man and a young woman standing together. Both of them are watching Gray with similar angry looks on their faces.

"Who are they?" I wonder out loud.

Kee and James both follow my gaze to the top floor.

"Hmmm, maybe they are the owners?"

"Perhaps," James responds, following their gaze to Gray, who is making her way around the dancefloor.

"They seem to be extra interested in your beau, Hannah."

"I know, it's weird, right?"

"Maybe now is a good time to get out of here. I don't like those two, and we don't need any trouble."

"James is right, Hannah. We should leave."

I nod in agreement. We settle the bill and gather our belongings. The young woman is gone from the balcony, but the man is still there, and I swear he's looking at me.

CHAPTER 31

Gray

I spot Kee and James ushering Hannah out of the bar and feel some of my body's tension disappear. I don't trust Kiera, and nothing scares me more than Kiera getting ahold of Hannah. There's no telling what she would do. It's best if Hannah never comes back here, especially now that Dimitri and Kiera have seen us together.

Hannah and I reconnected tonight. I'm hesitant to be hopeful that she's still into me and that we can pick up where we left off. And I know I shouldn't pursue her, but I can't get her out of my mind. I need her in every way.

If I proceed with this, though, I need to be extra cautious of Kiera and Dimitri. Especially given that Hannah's dad is the D.A. investigating Dimitri. She doesn't know that yet, and I don't want her to know I'm working for the biggest crime boss in the city. I can't let her find that out.

The rest of the night is uneventful, which is surprising. I'm still waiting for Kiera or Dimitri to call me to the office to reprimand me for leaving my station and dancing with a patron. Two things that we are never allowed to do. I know I'll be punished for breaking the rules. Not knowing the punishment and when it comes puts me on edge.

The last time I broke the rules, I received this lovely little scar running down the left side of my face. This time it feels much bigger and worse, and I'm scared to think about what they might do. It wasn't even a big mistake, just a tiny error in judgment.

I feel the panic creeping in as Marcus and I do our final checks and close the club for the night. It starts in my chest and slowly expands throughout the rest of my body, making it harder and harder to breathe.

I stop and double over for a minute, putting my hands on my knees, trying to calm myself and draw a deep breath.

"You alright, kid?" Marcus comes over, putting a hand between my shoulders and rubbing the tension out of them in soothing circles.

"Yeah, I just…I need a minute to catch my breath, is all."

"Hey, maybe they'll let it go." There's a small ounce of hope in his voice, but the doubt and nervousness drown it.

"Right, maybe they'll let it go," I repeat to him, drawing a deep breath and standing up. I flashback to the knife, slicing through the skin above and below my eye for a moment. The feeling of it, the burn as the skin splits. The panic grows, and I double over again.

"It'll be okay, kid. Let's get the fuck out of here and try to forget about it."

Nodding, I stand up again and straighten my jacket and tie. Find comfort in the things I know and the things I can control.

"Take a breath. I'll walk with you to your bike."

"Thanks, Marcus."

"Maybe you should be thinking about dancing with your doctor tonight and hold onto that, and you never know, maybe Kiera has grown out of her ways, and nothing will happen."

"I hope so."

Walking into the early morning and out of Midnight, I draw a deep breath of air and let the city soothe my troubled soul.

I danced with Hannah tonight.

A small smile touches my lips as Marcus and I reach my bike.

"It was pretty great, Marcus." I can't keep the smile off my face.

"Good, I'm glad you got to have a moment like that with her. Not to rain on your parade, but you should probably tell her to stay away from Midnight for a while. That will be best for both of you, don't you think?"

"I agree." The thought of Hannah disappearing again for weeks and months hurts my chest. "I'll call her tomorrow and explain why she needs to stay away from this place…and probably away from me for a while."

I missed her while we were apart, and tonight brought my feelings for her back to the surface.

"I know it's rough, Gray, but it's for the best. We both know that, and I bet Hannah will understand."

Nodding, I put my helmet on. I can't express to Marcus how important he is to me and how, even though he annoys the shit out of me, I don't think I would have survived this long at Midnight without him.

"Thanks, Marcus. I don't know what I would do without you."

"Probably get in less trouble!" he says with a light shove.

Starting my bike, I give him a final wave as I head home, letting the cool early dawn air wash away the grime of Midnight.

CHAPTER 32

Hannah

"Gray? Hello?" It's the next day, and it's the early afternoon. Why would Gray be calling me?

"Hey, Hannah. I need to talk to you about something. Would it be possible to meet up to grab lunch somewhere?"

Gray's voice sounds different. Melancholy.

"What's going on?"

"It would be best to tell you in person. There's a café not far from your house, Café Diem. Could you meet me there at two?"

"Yeah, it's no problem. I'll see you there."

Hanging up, I look up from the kitchen table at Kee and James, watching me.

"What was that about?" James asks, his voice coated in disgust.

"James, what is your problem with Gray? Has she done something?"

James and Kee look at one another, but neither answers my question.

"Gray wants to meet at two at Café Diem. I'm going, so you two can either get on board, or I'll be going by myself."

"Just take it easy, Hannah. We didn't say you couldn't go." Kee tries to ease the tension filling the room between James and me.

"I just don't understand what the two of you have against Gray. Do you know something about her that I don't?"

They exchange looks again.

"If you know something, you should tell me. I can ask her about it."

Shaking his head, James steps back and raises his hands, "I think it's something we can talk about later. Why don't you get ready, and I'll bring the car around."

I can tell they are hiding something, and my frustration and impatience grow. I want to say more, but James is already walking away.

Kee tightly smiles at me before following him. "I'll let you know when the car's ready."

A few minutes later, Kee's voice rings out from the first floor of my house, "Hannah! We're clear it's time to go if you want to be on time!"

Grabbing my jacket, I rush to meet Kee and James. It's hard to keep the smile off my face, even with the two of them acting weird.

I'm going to see Gray, and I'm so excited I feel like I'm going on a first date.

It was just lunch, but it was more than that. I hadn't been out for lunch with anyone since this whole thing started and getting to finally go out again and be with Gray made it much more meaningful.

"Alright, let's go," I say as I hop into the car.

Kee shuts the door, and I glance at James' profile. He looks just as surly as always, but there's a hint of something else that I just can't place.

"James, I wish you and Kee would just tell me what's happening. I can handle it."

Looking at me in the review mirror, James doesn't respond, he simply puts the car in drive, and we're off to meet Gray.

CHAPTER 33

Gray

Even though I know I shouldn't pursue things with Hannah, I can't stop wanting to see her again and again.

At least today, I don't have to worry about Kiera seeing us. Kiera and Dimitri rarely venture into this part of the city, especially in the daytime. I'm confident I can spend the afternoon with Hannah without anyone seeing or interrupting us. We can enjoy simple things like lunch together.

I haven't felt this way for someone in a long time, and I'm uncertain about what to do with it.

I always do what I know I should, what's right. But when it comes to Hannah, I can't convince myself that letting her go is right. I know she has Kee and James, but the desire to keep her safe and close to me drives me to make choices I know I shouldn't. I'm overwhelmed and thrown off balance by what I feel for her; all I can think about is the next time I'll be able to see her.

The thought of this date has been keeping me together since last night. It saved my mind from what Dimitri and Kiera might be planning and kept my eyes focused on what could be. Is it wise to turn a blind eye to Kiera and Dimitri? Most definitely not, but I just need a moment of living and feeling something real. I need to be reminded that a world exists outside of Midnight. That there are good people in the world.

I see Hannah's car pulling up and standing from my seat outside the café. I've picked one of my favorite spots. It's a quaint café with indoor/outdoor space, and the weather is perfect for a warm cup of coffee outside. Sitting exposed outside isn't the safest option, but I know Hannah will like it, and the weather is just too nice to pass up.

Kee and Hannah exit the car as James pulls away to find parking.

I can't help but smile as she walks towards me. She looks perfectly dressed in a sweater, light jacket, and fitted jeans. She couldn't look cuter. Her strawberry-blonde hair is pulled into a sloppy ponytail that bobs with every step she takes. I fight the urge to grab and kiss her on the street. My palms itch with the need. Instead, I put my hands in my pockets and avoid bursting into a big idiotic smile.

Hannah's smiling as she walks towards me, and I start moving towards her when I see something flash out of the corner of my eye.

"Hannah!"

CHAPTER 34

Hannah

I'm so focused on walking to Gray that I don't see the man at first. He isn't dressed in all black with a mask on like I thought he would be. No, he's wearing regular clothes and looks like a guy on his way to lunch. Except he's not. He's here for something else. He's here to ruin my fucking day.

"Hannah!" Gray shouts right as the man lunges at me, throwing herself at him in the same instant.

Kee is also moving, pushing me back while reaching out to stop his hand.

I can't see what he has in his hand, but I glimpse something shiny before Gray is there, blocking my view.

Kee grabs me and pulls me away, and I can't see what's happening. I can hear the tearing of cloth and hissing of breaths, grunting, and a gasp before being pushed into the car that I never saw coming back for me.

It all happens so fast, and it's all over before I know what's happened.

I'm in the back of the car. Gray is on the ground with the man pinned under her knee. Onlookers gather from the cafe, and James is on the phone calling the authorities.

"Kee, Kee, is Gray okay? I need to get out and check on her."

I feel frantic, and I'm scared. Scared that Gray has been hurt and that she's bleeding out on the street and no one is helping her.

"Please, Kee, James, I need to get out and check on Gray."

"Hannah, I need you to just wait a few more minutes for the police to get here. I can see Gray, and she looks fine. She's subdued the attacker and seems to be okay. Just wait a few more minutes."

"Are you sure? I thought I saw a knife."

"I'm sure, Hannah. Please just trust me."

My heart is racing out of my chest, and I don't know when I've ever been more afraid for someone in my life.

I don't know if it's possible to fall in love with someone shortly after meeting them, but I think I have. I don't know when it happened, but I know that I haven't had this feeling before, and I would do anything to ensure that Gray is okay and safe.

Anything.

CHAPTER 35

Gray

'm unsteady even though I'm kneeling on the back of Hannah's attacker. I never would have thought that someone would try to attack Hannah in broad daylight. I can't believe my eyes as I look down at the man under my knee. I know him, and he knows me.

It's one of Dimitri's guys. "Why are you here, Roy? Who sent you after Hannah?"

"I should be asking you the same thing, Gray. What are you doing here with that woman?"

"What do you know about 'that woman'? I need you to talk to me, Roy. If you want my help, you need to tell me what the hell is going on."

He struggles under my knee as sirens pick up in the distance.

"If you're not here because Dimitri sent you, then you don't need to know." Roy spits on the ground as he squirms under my knee. I put more pressure on him until he stops moving.

"Goddamn it, Roy! Just fucking tell me what Dimitri wants with her!" I'm trying to keep my cool, but I can feel the panic building. "Does this have to do with the D.A. investigation? Are they investigating Dimitri?"

Ray stops moving, "How do you know about that?"

Fuck, this is what I was worried about when James and Kee mentioned D.A. Winters.

"Did Dimitri tell you about it?" Silence is my best weapon here. I need to learn as much as possible, and Roy seems to know what's happening. Hopefully, Roy will take my silence for confirmation and keep talking.

"Dimitri's trying to make it go away by threatening the guy's family. I was supposed to scare her and get the message across. Not anything serious."

"Not anything serious? Roy! You came at her with a knife, and now I can't let you go. They've called the cops."

"Come on, Gray. Just let me up. We can make it look good."

Shit. What should I do? If I let him go, it'll give me an in with Dimitri. If he gets picked up, Dimitri will bail him out, and then he'll rat me out to Dimitri. Can I convince him that this is part of Dimitri's plan?

"Here's the deal, Roy. Dimitri asked me to stay with her, track her movements, and keep her close. I'm not sure why I wasn't told about your plans today, but I need to stay with them to keep Dimitri up to date on what's going on. If I let you go, no matter how good we make it look, they will suspect something is happening. I'm sorry, man, but I must let them take you in."

"Dimitri told you to stay with her?" It doesn't sound like he believes me at all.

"Yes, no one knows, just Dimitri. Can you keep your cool and stay calm until we bail you out?"

Roy nods into the ground giving in to the plan.

I might be able to pull this off.

CHAPTER 36

Hannah

"Can I get out of the car now? Please." I don't wait for either of them to answer, but instead, I push the door open and get out, rushing over to where Gray is standing with the police officers.

I pass the spot on the ground where Gray and the man were just moments ago.

I try to steal my heart and steady my breath as I approach Gray. I can hear Kee following closely behind me.

"Did he say anything about why he attacked your friend?"

"He mentioned an ongoing investigation about the D.A., but that was about it."

"Do you know what that's about?"

"We'll fill you in." James' voice comes from behind me as I reach for Gray.

"Are you alright? Did you get hurt?"

"I'm okay, it's alright. I'm alright." Gray runs her left hand down my face before grasping my right hand with her left.

"You're cut!" I can't keep the panic from my voice as I catch a glimpse of a cut in the right arm of her jacket.

"Let me see. I said let me see!" Grabbing Gray's arm, I push the jacket sleeve out of the way to reveal a tanned tattooed arm.

No wound.

"I told you I was fine. My jacket, on the other hand, not so much."

Gray smiles at me, and something in her eyes makes me think she's also fallen for me. Just maybe.

"I'm not a fan of knives," I whisper, running my hand up and down the area of Gray's arm where the cut would have been.

"Me either," Gray says, taking my hand in hers. "How about we skip lunch and get you home?"

"James can pick us up some food, and we can have our date from my place."

"That sounds perfect." Gray smiles, gently caressing my cheek and pushing a loose strand of hair behind my ear.

CHAPTER 37

Gray

"I'd like to look at your arm again," Hannah says as we walk into the sunroom.

"Hannah, you've looked at my arm at least six times. I'm fine, I promise."

I look into her green eyes and notice for the first time the different greens and how they make her eyes look like a rolling field of green blowing in the wind.

"You promise you're okay?" she whispers softly.

"Yeah, I'm okay. Promise." My voice seems stuck in my throat, and I can't seem to make it get louder. It's as if the world will shatter around me if I talk too loudly or move too quickly. The spell would be broken, and that's the last thing I want to do.

"You're sure?" she whispers back, leaning in.

"I'm sure." I lean forward and meet her lips halfway to mine. It's a soft kiss, gentle with undertones of want and desire. I bring my left hand to cup her cheek and neck and deepen the kiss. Hearing her slight gasp makes me kiss her harder. I want her. Forgetting about Dimitri, Kiera, and Roy, I lean further into my kiss with Hannah. Nipping her bottom lip as I pull away to catch my breath.

"Shit."

She's flushed, every inch of her exposed skin is dusted in pink, and her lips reddened and swollen from my kisses.

Breathing is hard as she continues to steal the air from my lungs. I want to kiss her again.

"We should eat, and then we can… continue…if you'd like." She glances up shyly with a knowing smile.

"Deal."

When we make it into the kitchen for a late lunch, our lips are red and swollen from kissing.

I catch Kee exchanging a look with Hannah, which gives me pause. It's as if she's cautioning her with her eyes.

I wonder what that's about?

We're finally getting our date, albeit at Hannah's house. I just want to be close to her for as long as possible. I will take whatever I can get.

Luckily, James and Kee have finally left us alone in the dining room, giving Hannah and me a chance to get to know each other better. After all, we've only spent a little time together and always seem to get interrupted.

This is nice. Normal. Something I haven't experienced in a long time. Being with someone without watching my back makes me feel like I can let down my guard. Be me and not have to put on a show or any walls.

"Are you enjoying the food?"

I've been quiet for too long, caught up in my ponderings of being myself around Hannah, and left her in silence.

"Mmmm, it's delicious. I haven't had Chinese in a long time. It's hitting the spot."

"It's one of my favorite places. I probably eat there way too often. I always get the Sweet and Sour chicken."

"You shouldn't do that. Going to the same places, someone could learn your routines."

"I know, I know. Kee and James say the same thing, but I can't help it. It's the only food that brings me comfort after a rough shift.

There's nothing better than some tasty crab Rangoon and some sweet and sour chicken!"

"Well, if you order it occasionally, you're mixing it up enough."

"Please don't lecture me. I've got James and Kee to do that for me."

"Noted. No more lecturing from me." I smile, bringing another forkful of food to my mouth.

Smiling back at me, Hannah takes a sip from her wine and moves from the chair at the end of the table to the chair next to me.

I'm so caught up in her that I forget why I wanted to meet up with her in the first place.

CHAPTER 38

Hannah

Gray seems quiet, and I'm worried about her. Given what has happened today, I don't know if it's that or if she's having doubts about everything.

"Are you alright?" I ask, sitting in the chair next to her.

"Mmmhmm, I'm just…enjoying this. Taking it all in."

"Taking in having Chinese food?" I can't keep the smile from my face. It's something so mundane and ordinary.

"With you. Having Chinese food *with you*. I'm just taking it all in and enjoying it."

The smile slips from my face for a moment realizing that Gray hasn't had many opportunities to live their life as an average person would.

"I guess we'll have to do more fun, normal things," I say, reaching for Gray's hand.

Gray smiles at me, but it doesn't quite reach her eyes. Sadness lingers momentarily before she returns to the food in front of her.

"Chinese food was actually one of my mother's favorite dishes. She would order it all the time." Gray says, still looking down at her dish of beef and noodles.

"Oh, does she not eat it anymore?"

"I'm not sure. I haven't spoken to my parents in a long time. Years. I don't even know if they still live in the same place. They did the last time I contacted them."

"I'm sorry, Gray." It's the only thing I can think to say at that moment. "I know what it's like to have parents that aren't around and maybe don't approve of who you are."

"You do? I thought your dad was different. It seems he cares about you, with the security and everything."

"He's more worried about people finding out that he has a daughter, especially one that isn't straight! It would ruin his reputation, or at least that's what he thinks."

"That's terrible, Hannah. I'm sorry to hear that. I thought it was the opposite." Gray reaches across the table for my hand.

Reaching for her, I smile. "It's okay. It's been like this my whole life. It got worse when my mom passed away. That's when we really grew apart. He didn't know how to handle me and just shut down." I glance at our hands, smiling albeit a bit sadly.

"His loss. You've done really well for yourself, Hannah. You're a successful doctor and just bought your first house. That's pretty great."

"What about you, Gray? Would your parents be proud of you?" I can't help but ask it. I know Kee and James don't trust Gray and think that she's nothing but bad news. I want to prove them wrong.

"No, I don't think they would be. I've...done things, been a part of things that aren't good, Hannah. You should know that about me. I'm not...I'm not a good person like you are."

"I don't know if I believe that," I say, tightening my hand in hers before she can pull back. I want to keep her in the moment, keep Gray here with me.

"Hey, it's about time to call it a night," Kee says as she enters the room.

"Right, I forgot y'all have rules and routines around here that need to be followed." Gray goes to get up, we're still holding hands, and I don't want to let go.

"I think Gray is going to stay here tonight."

They all turn to stare at me. Gray's eyebrows rise in surprise.

"I am?"

"She is?"

"Yes. This is my home, and if I want someone to stay the night and they agree to it, then what's the problem?"

"No…no problem here. I'll let James know," Kee manages as she tries to hide her surprise.

"You'll stay the night, won't you?" I ask, turning to face Gray, who still seems confused about what just happened.

"Um. I mean…yes, if you want me to, I'd love to stay."

"Good, that's settled then. Are you still hungry?"

Gray looks fully at me. The change in her eyes lets me know she's finished with the meal yet still hungry for more.

The sensation starts in the middle of my chest, moving to my stomach and then my core. My breath hitches, and my body clenches with anticipation. I've never had a reaction to anyone like this before. My body seems to have a mind of its own. I've lost all control. I feel the blush rushing up my neck to my face.

Gray's hand follows the flush path, running her hand up my neck, chin, and cheek.

"Should we go upstairs?" Her voice is soft and tender even though there isn't anything delicate about it.

I can only nod, my throat too tight to get words through. She grips my hand a little tighter.

"Lead the way."

I nod again and start towards the stairs, my chest exploding with every step closer to my room.

CHAPTER 39

Gray

Staying the night was the last thing I thought would happen tonight, especially given how our date started. Yet, I am following Hannah up the stairs to her room.

My hand is tightly grasped in hers, our fingers intertwined. Rough and soft skin connected. My breath quickens with every step taken closer to her room. I'm having a hard time believing that this is actually happening. But I'm glad it is, Hannah is extraordinary, and I've never wanted someone as severely as I like her. I want her in every way. I want to be close to her, I want to hold her, I want to sit and talk with her about nothing of importance. I've fallen hard.

The upstairs of Hannah's house is nothing like the bare-bones house below. It's light and airy, with pops of color that show her personality. It's comfortable, soft, yet colorful, just like her. I take in as much as possible as she leads me to the bedroom at the end of the hall. Her room is spacious, with a large bed, a small writing desk, a bay window, an en suite, and a large walk-in closet. It looks like there are at least two other rooms on this floor. A guest room and an office.

There aren't any photos in the entire house, but there is art. Beautiful pieces of art throughout her home of all mediums and subject matter. Art is something that matters to her, that she enjoys and appreciates. I'll remember that for another time.

We walk into her bedroom, and Hannah turns, letting go of my hand and shutting the door behind her. Suddenly I'm unsure of what to do, I don't want to move too fast, and I don't want to overwhelm her with my desire.

To my surprise, Hannah takes the lead, pushing me gently back against the door before stopping our lips inches apart.

"I like you very much," she whispers, every word caressing my lips.

I lift her chin, looking into her eyes before following the soft curve of her nose to her lips. Leaning in, I press my lips to hers. Taking a deep breath and filling my lungs with her before pushing and deepening the kiss. Her lips part with a gasp as I kiss harder, my hands now cupping her face as she leans into me, pressing me harder into the door.

She pulls away, kissing my jawline, my ear lobe, and down my neck. Her hands run down my neck, chest, stomach, and up again as her mouth leaves burning trails of kisses before finding my lips again.

I hadn't expected her to be bold, and I'm happy for her to take the lead. I'll follow wherever she wants to take us.

Hannah's kisses become frantic as her hands find their way to the hem of my shirt. Tugging at it, she pulls it over my head. She's kissing down my neck, to the scars on my chest, which she peppers with kisses before moving to the waist of my pants.

Fuck.

I can barely keep my wits about me as she assaults all of my senses with her kisses and hands. I nearly pass out as she flicks her tongue over my stomach, making me clench involuntarily. My body is no longer my own. It's possessed by my need for Hannah. She's in complete control, and I'll do anything she wants.

Hannah continues kissing and exploring my body with her mouth and hands before returning to my lips. It takes me a few moments to register that she's asked me a question. I'm entirely out of my mind and breathless.

"Wh…what?" I manage through the fog.

"Come take a shower with me?"

I manage a nod as she leads me to the en suite.

Holy shit.

CHAPTER 40

Hannah

'm enjoying myself way too much. I love making Gray squirm, making her want. At this point, she's partially dressed, and I'm still fully clothed. I like being in control and that she's letting me take control. It makes me feel comfortable and safe. It makes me want her even more.

"Come take a shower with me?" It's a whisper, and it takes Gray a few moments to respond.

She opens her eyes and lifts her head off the wall, and I can see her returning to herself enough to answer me.

Nodding, she pushes off the wall, and I take her hand, leading her to the en suite. I've never showered with anyone before, not in this way, and I'm nervous, but the desire is making me bold. I also want to take all of her in. Gray's body is impressive and muscular, yet she's still feminine in all the right ways and places. A mix of masculine and feminine that tingles all of the correct areas of my brain and body.

I'm buzzing with excitement as we head into the bathroom.

I turn on the faucet letting the water warm as I take off my shirt, raising my eyes haltingly to meet Gray's.

The heat in her eyes makes me step forward, reaching for her, our bodies meeting as we catch each other's excited gasps between our lips. Gray quickly removes my bra, her right hand caressing my breast as she kisses my neck. I see myself in the mirror and have no idea who this person is. My skin is stained pink, my lips plump and red from kissing, my strawberry blonde hair disheveled, glassy-eyed, and wrapped around the most beautiful being I've ever met.

Gray trails kisses from my neck down to my breasts, pausing to linger on my nipples long enough to elicit a groan before moving to the next. My hands are in her hair, guiding and letting her do as she pleases. Kissing her way back to my mouth, her hands are busy undoing my pants. I reach down, fumbling with her belt, button, and zipper. We undress each other as we continue to kiss before stepping into the shower.

I turn to face the water and press into Gray, feeling her body wrap around mine as she cups my breasts from behind. I lean my head back, letting the warm water run down my body and taking in the feeling of Gray's hands following the water flow from my breasts down my belly. Gray kisses my neck, nibbles my ear lobe and turns my head so she can kiss me as her left hand continues to explore my body. Caressing, pinching, touching all of the throbbing places on my body, making me moan into her kisses.

I let myself go and give myself over to the sensation of our wet bodies.

Pulling Gray into me and kissing her hard, I turn us so the water hits Gray's back. Gray continues her assault on my body, her lips finding their way to my breasts, taking one then the other in her mouth, sucking, nibbling, licking. Creating sensations along with her fingers that drive me to the edge.

"Gray..." her name escapes with a groan as I get closer.

Gray moves to her knees, turning me so my back is to the shower wall. I grip the rack there as she lifts my right leg over her shoulder. I grab Gray's short hair as her tongue plays over me, licking, sucking, and pleasing me until I can't breathe.

"Gray!" I can't stop but lean into her and grasp her tighter as I feel myself tightening. She applies more pressure, and I gasp. Gray stays where she is, gently letting me down from the spiraling experience. She lowers my leg, kissing the inside of my thighs, before finding her way back to my breasts, neck, and mouth.

I can't breathe or feel my legs, yet I can feel everything all at once, all at the same time. Gasping for breath, I sag into her as she pins me to the wall, gently kissing my body, holding me up with hers.

I have no idea how long we've been in the shower, and the events of the day seem to hit me, and I'm suddenly exhausted.

"Should we get out?" Gray whispers.

I nod into her shoulder, still clinging to her.

CHAPTER 41

Gray

lift Hannah from the shower. Grabbing the towel from the rack, I wrap it around her. She's all soft pinks and loose limbs. Grabbing a second towel, I wrap her hair.

Hannah's quiet, sleepy, sated, and barely functioning. Finding a third towel in the nearby closet, I finish drying myself and wrap the towel around my waist before helping Hannah dry herself off.

"Tired?" I ask her, chuckling softly, as I take the towel from her hair, drying it for her.

She nods, looking up at me from dew-dusted lashes, "Very," she mumbles with a happy smile.

"Good, you'll sleep well then." I finish drying her hair, and we walk naked from the bathroom.

"PJs?"

Sitting on the bed, she points to the dresser in the corner, "Top drawer."

I open the drawer pulling out an oversized shirt which I hand to her before turning back to find something for myself. I see some large shorts that look like they'll fit. Stepping into them, I turn back to the bed to find Hannah under the covers and out cold.

I return to the dresser and find a shirt to wear to get a glass of water downstairs. Reaching the kitchen, I find the cabinet with the glasses and grab one.

"Need help?" I nearly shit myself as Kee comes into the kitchen.

"Jesus Christ! Kee, you surprised the shit out of me." I lean against the counter, catching my breath as Kee comes in, taking the glass from me and filling it at the sink beside me.

"I need you to know something, Gray. Hannah is more than just a client to us, she's important, and James and I care greatly for her." Kee pauses with the glass in hand. "James and I know more about you than you think, and if at any moment we think that her being with you is putting her in more danger, we will pull the plug on this thing you have going on. Do you understand?" Looking at Kee, she seems like a different person. Her bubbly personality is gone; I can see she's dead serious. James and Kee must have done their research into my background. Given what Kee has just said, it's the only thing that would make sense.

"Understood," I say, looking her in the eye. "I will do my damnedest to not hurt her and to keep her safe."

Satisfied, Kee nods, passing the glass of cool water into my warm hand.

"Don't fuck this up, Gray. She really likes you." With that, she wanders out of the kitchen.

Hannah is still out and hasn't moved since I left. I crawl into the bed beside her, relaxing and letting sleep nibble at my consciousness. Hannah mumbles softly, then moves closer to me, draping herself over my body before settling and drifting off again.

This all feels brand-new, like it's the first time I've experienced any of this, and I want it to stay like this for as long as possible.

Sleep tugs at the corners of my mind, and I drift off.

CHAPTER 42

Hannah

As I wake up, I forget what happened last night before it all comes rushing back, and I find myself wrapped around a sleeping Gray.

Holy shit.

Gray seems to be sleeping soundly, giving me a moment to look closely at her without feeling shy or awkward.

Gray's features look so different. All the sharp angles are relaxed. The space between her brows isn't furrowed. Even her scar seems softer. Her scar. How did she get it? What happened? Who gave it to her?

What exactly does she do at the club besides running security?

My gut tells me Gray is involved in much more than just helping with the club.

I run my hand down her face, gently caressing the scar. Gray jerks awake, grabbing my wrist so hard that it makes me jump and gasp from the pain. She blinks, looking from me to my wrist, which she's still gripping, before letting go.

"S...sorry, you surprised me." Gray's voice is laden with sleep and shame.

"No, I'm sorry, I shouldn't have..." She's turning from me as I talk, rolling to her side and then sitting up, her back to me.

"It's okay. I wake up like that sometimes." I reach out slowly towards Gray, laying my hand on her bare shoulder, which relaxes under my touch. Moving to sit behind her, I continue to caress her shoulders, moving my left hand to her other shoulder as I kiss the back of her neck.

Gray relaxes back into me, releasing a deep breath and the slightest of moans.

"I'll be more careful in how I wake you next time," I whisper as I kiss and nibble her earlobe.

"I think I can handle that." Gray leans harder into me, and I wrap my arms around her neck and let her settle back into me.

"Where did you get your scar?" I ask, still peppering kisses along her shoulders.

The tension returns.

"If you don't want to talk about it, we don't have to."

"I pissed off the wrong people and paid the price for it," Gray whispers, looking down at her clasped hands.

"Which people?" I have a sinking feeling that I already know what she will say.

"Dimitri and his daughter Kiera. Which is why I don't think you should come to the club anymore. It's not safe there for you."

"And it is for you? Safe?"

Gray turns slightly, looking me in the eye, her face is stern and serious, and I know she means what she's saying.

"I need you to stay away from Midnight. It's what's best for both of us. Kiera is very…possessive of me, and Dimitri doesn't like us mingling with patrons. If they suspect anything, let's just say this won't be my only scar." Gray's blue eyes are darker and more searching as she looks at me.

I know I should agree to stay away, but Midnight was our place. It's where we met and one of the only places that I know to go to see Gray.

"Okay, I'll stay away from Midnight, but I need something from you in return."

"Anything," Gray says, her eyes drifting to my lips and back to my eyes again.

"More time. I want to get to know you better. You're full of secrets, and I don't feel like I know you at all. I want to know who you really are. Not who you are at Club Midnight."

Gray pauses and something in her eyes changes. "I'll try my best to let you in, Hannah, but it's going to take me a while to work up to it."

Nodding, I reach for her face, cupping it and leaning in to kiss her slightly chapped lips.

"Should we get some breakfast?"

"No, let's stay like this for a little longer," I say, running my hands over her bare chest.

Her reply is soft and soothing, like the early morning light filtering through the bay windows of my bedroom.

If only we could stay like this.

Gray grasps my hands in hers as if reading my mind, saying, "Do you have to work today?"

"Yeah, my shift starts in a couple of hours."

"Hmmm, that's no good. You can't call out?"

I can't help but chuckle. "And what would we do all day if I were to do that?" I can feel the growl move from Gray's chest to her throat as she turns on me quickly, pinning me to the bed. "I can think of a few things." The arched eyebrow makes me giggle as she pretends to bite my neck while I squirm, trying to escape.

"Gray! We have to get up!" I squirm, giggling more as she nips my neck, following it with kisses.

"Gray!" I cry again.

"Okay, okay, you're right. We should get up, and we should definitely take another shower." Throwing a wink, she reaches down and lifts me over her shoulder! It's as if I weigh nothing.

"What are you doing?!"

"We're taking a shower, I told you."

"Gray! Really!" I say. "Fine, but no funny business, deal?"

"Deal."

CHAPTER 43

Gray

I can't keep the smile off my face as I leave Hannah's and head back to mine.

I haven't felt like this in such a long time. I'm unsure if I even have the words to describe my feelings.

My chest is full and tight but in the best way possible.

It feels good to be with Hannah, but she also makes me forget, which isn't good. She makes me forget that I live in a dark world and she's in a world of light. I have to keep her from letting the dark in. I don't want her to be soiled by the world that I live in.

I don't want it to touch her more than it already is. I have to figure out what's happening with this investigation and how Dimitri is involved. I need to fill Marcus in on what happened as well. He'll know what to do about Ray and how to navigate everything.

It's Saturday, and we'll both be at Midnight this evening, so I can work through it once I arrive. Maybe I'll be lucky, Dimitri will be gone, and I'll have a bit more time to get my thoughts together.

* * *

This is the worst possible thing that could happen tonight. Kiera was waiting for me to show up tonight, and it's been downhill from there. I'm on Kiera duty and didn't even get a chance to talk with Marcus.

I have difficulty focusing on Kiera, paranoid that Hannah will walk into Midnight at any minute and see us dancing. I won't know how to explain everything if she sees Kiera grinding against my thigh on the dancefloor.

Not to mention, Roy got out on bail today, which means he's likely spoken with or will be speaking with Dimitri soon. My stomach turns as the anxiety hits.

I am so fucked.

"Who are you looking for?" Kiera shouts over the music, grabbing my chin with one hand as the other grips my shoulder.

"No one. Just thought it was someone I knew, but it's not." Kiera is possessive and violent. Volatile in all the worst ways possible. She can't find out about Hannah. Who knows what she'll do to Hannah or me if she does.

"You should only be looking at me. I'm here for you, ya know." Her eyes are glued to my lips like a predator watching its prey before pouncing. Her sharp gel nails dig into the flesh of my cheek before running down to my neck. She applies pressure to my neck as she finds the rhythm and continues to undulate over my thigh.

I know a kiss is coming, and I can do nothing to escape it. If I resist, Kiera will tell Dimitri, and that punishment would be far worse than the kiss, although not by much.

"I think I need some water!" I shout over the music leaning away from the incoming kiss.

Kiera's eyes flash, and her nails dig deeper into my flesh.

Kiera grabs my hand and leads me to the back bar. I'm technically supposed to be her security. Still, everyone in Midnight knows not to mess with Kiera, so I have little to worry about and let her do as she pleases.

Walking to the back bar, Kiera nods to the new bartender, and he hands her a bottle of water.

"Here you go, love." Kiera smiles, opening the bottle and handing it to me as she smiles deviously.

I go to take a drink, pausing for a moment before it hits my lips. She wouldn't put anything in this, would she? The bottle was closed when she got it from the bartender. She didn't have time to slip anything into it.

Kiera is known to use drug cocktails of her own making to make her conquests more accommodating.

I cautiously take a sip of the drink. It didn't taste weird, and the bottle was closed. I take another tentative drink.

* * *

My body is on fire, and I can't seem to focus or think clearly. I know I've been drugged, but it's a distant thought compared to the burning and throbbing of my body. My flesh is hot and thrumming with desire. I can't seem to keep my eyes open and stumble down the hall as someone leads me by my hand down the darkened corridor.

Where am I, and who is with me? Why do I want them so badly?

I'm vaguely aware of a door opening and find myself pushed against the wall. There are hands everywhere. They undo my shirt, jacket, belt, buttons, and zipper. Everything is happening too fast.

"S...stop." I don't sound right in my ears. My throat is so dry, the words slurred. I'm so thirsty, so hot. This needs to stop. It's not right. This doesn't seem right.

"Stop!" I manage to force the words out.

Kiera laughs. "I know you want me as badly as I want you. You just need a little encouragement to make a move." Her laughter pinballs through my foggy brain.

"No...stop, please." She giggles as she runs her hands down my bare chest, to my waist, then lower, cupping me. She presses into me, undulating. I'm burning. I can't breathe. I pant as the fire rips through my body, and the throbbing grows.

I push her from me as she kisses my neck, running her burning kisses up my jaw and then to my lips. She tastes of whiskey, cigarettes, and sourness.

I can't seem to raise my arms. I have no control over my body as the drugs in my system make it react to her pursuits. I hate that my body reacts, throbbing more as she grinds into me.

I'm weak and can't do anything to stop her. I'm helpless, and it's something I've never felt before. It's getting harder to breathe, and I feel myself falling further into the darkness of the drugs.

I'm half standing, half slumped against the wall next to the door, and Kiera is all over me. I'm aware enough to know that my shirt is completely open, and my pants undone, and I can feel that my skin is flushed bright red. I can't seem to focus my eyes as they swim in my head, trying to find a focal point. No matter how hard I try to fight back, whatever Kiera put in my water prevents me from doing so.

"What the fuck do you think you're doing?!" Marcus' voice rips through my shattered consciousness, and I dully watch as he grabs Kiera by the upper arm and pulls her off me.

My legs give out, and I slide to the floor. My breathing is heavy and labored, and my body is covered in sweat. I can feel every drop of it as it runs down my fiery skin.

"What did you give her, and how much? Tell me. Now!" Marcus' voice is booming, and I jerk back to awareness for the briefest of moments, long enough to see him and Kiera mere inches away as he tries to get her to tell him what she's done.

Kiera spits the words at Marcus, rage clear on her face as her plans are interrupted. "Fuck you! Leave me alone. She wants it. Look at her!"

"Get the fuck out of here before I lose my temper," Marcus spits back, pointing to the door.

Kiera sneers, "Wait until my dad hears about this." She walks out.

"Gray, hey. Can you open your eyes?" Marcus touches my face and neck lightly. His rough, callused hands are cool against my skin.

I'm burning.

"Fuck, I know you don't want to involve her, but I don't know what to do. I'm going to call Hannah. She's the only doctor I know that can treat you off the books."

I hear the words as Marcus says them, and a small part of my brain still understands them, but I have nothing left in my body to give.

I let the drugs take hold and sink into unconsciousness.

CHAPTER 44

Hannah

"Hannah! Hannah, it's Marcus. I'm on Gray's phone. Listen, please meet me in the club's back alley. Just drive right up to the back door!" Marcus' booming voice is frantic, and he isn't giving me time to comprehend what's happening.

Something's wrong. I can tell by the tone of his voice.

"Marcus, what's happening? Is Gray okay?"

James looks at me from his station at the living room window. Wordlessly, taking in the situation, he moves closer, taking his phone out and sending a text to Kee, I assume.

I pull the phone away and put it on speakerphone, reading the request on James' face before he can ask.

"It's Gray, Kiera drugged her, and I think she might be overdosing."

"What?" I can't seem to understand what he's saying to me. The sudden thrumming of my pulse in my ears makes me feel like I might pass out.

Kee pushes the front door open and looks from James to me as we stand on either side of the hallway. My phone held out between us.

"I need you to come to the club now. I think Gray is overdosing," he repeats, taking a deep breath and letting it out over the line.

"I don't know what Kiera gave her, but she's hot and breathing weird. I can't get her to wake up. You're the only doctor I know that can treat Gray off the books, and it *has* to be off the books, Hannah."

Marcus pauses again. I can hear him breathing heavily between muttering soothing words to Gray.

Heart racing, I look from James to Kee.

"We have to go," I say. "Marcus, it will take a few minutes. In the meantime, I need you to get a washcloth or something, wet it down with cold water, and put it on her neck. Try to keep her cool. Maybe try to get her to drink some water if you can."

James opens his mouth to protest, but I'm already moving with Kee towards the door.

"James, you're either coming with, or we're going without you," I say, feeling bold in my desire to get to Gray and help her.

James doesn't protest. He falls in line behind us, and we head to the car. "Kee, radio the others and let them know what's going on and that we'll bring one more back with us," James says, opening the back door for me as Kee gets in the driver's seat.

The ten-minute drive feels like it takes forever. I can't keep my nerves in check and find myself picking my nails and bouncing my leg to eliminate my nervous energy.

Pulling up to Club Midnight, I don't know what I was expecting, but what I found was far worse than anything I had envisioned.

Gray is slumped between Marcus and Luke. Her shirt is unbuttoned, along with the button of her slacks. Her skin is flushed and sweaty, yet her face is pale. I can see her working hard to breathe.

"Help me get her in the car," I say before we've even pulled to a complete stop. "We need to cool her down fast. Isn't there something in the club we can use?"

"We can't. Not here. You need to take her somewhere else," Marcus says, moving Gray towards the vehicle.

"What? We don't have time!" I feel a slight twinge of nervousness and panic flutter through me.

"*If you stay here, you're all in danger,*" Marcus stresses every word, and I can see he's worried for Gray and all of us. "You have to move her now."

"Okay, Kee, James, help them get Gray into the car."

Kee and James move, each taking an arm and lifting Gray from Marcus and Luke's grasp. Her head lulls from side to side, and she appears out of it now.

Gray's half walking, half being dragged, and a groan escapes from her chapped and swollen lips. James helps brace Gray as Kee lowers her into the backseat of the car.

That bitch did this to her. Made her this sick and made her lips swollen without her consent.

I'm furious, and my anger pushes my worry aside.

"I want to know everything about that woman," I mutter to Kee.

"Oh, don't worry, I'll find out everything, but right now, we need to focus on getting you and Gray out of here."

I nod, and James motions for us to get in the car. I slide into the back seat, and Kee tries to lower Gray into the back seat as gently as she can, but Gray is deadweight and flops ungracefully onto the seat.

I elevate her head on my lap and check her pulse. Her heart is racing, her breathing is ragged, and her eyes flutter as if she's in a nightmare. Gray continues to groan as the drug races through her system. God only knows what she's feeling.

"James, please drive faster. As fast as you can. Kee, when we arrive, I need you to fill the downstairs guest room bath with cold water, and James, can you grab my medkit once we get Gray inside?"

"Copy," they both respond. We're all in business mode. Gray is mine, she's one of us, and her well-being is a top priority right now, and everyone is on board to ensure that she makes it out alive.

As we pull up to the house, Kee jumps out to check the house and get the room ready while James and I pull Gray from the vehicle and head into the place.

Gray is on fire. Her skin is hot to the touch and clammy.

"James, we need to hurry. I'm worried. She's burning up."

"I know, I know, we're almost there."

Dragging Gray into the house, Kee is already waiting at the guest bedroom door. James and I carry Gray into the room, lowering her into the cold water of the tub.

Gray briefly returns to awareness, eyes opening and gasping awake, before sliding back into oblivion, letting the drugs pull her back under.

"Gray! Gray! I need you to wake up. Can you open your eyes?" I try to bring her back by rubbing my knuckles into her sternum, but her only response is minor. Groaning, she sinks further into the cool water, struggling to open her eyes.

"Hot, too hot…" Gray struggles to get the words out, fighting through the fog.

"I know. You should start to feel better soon. The water should help."

"Here's the medkit. Do you need anything else?" James drops the kit at the door.

"No, I'll take it from here. Keep your phone close if we need to take her to a hospital."

James leaves. It's only the two of us now.

"I …don't feel right."

"I know. I'm sorry there isn't more I can do for you. We have to let the drug run its course."

Gray's hands move from her side, one running from her neck to her chest, then down her flat stomach to the waist of her slacks.

Given the type of drugs likely used, I know what's about to happen. They're designed to make a person completely unaware of everything while consuming them with the need for pleasure.

"Help…me…" Her voice is pleading, riding the line between pleasure and pain. She struggles to undo her pants.

Swallowing hard, I reach down, unbuttoning and unzipping her slacks. As I start to retract my hand, she reaches for it. Holding it tightly and resting it on her stomach above her waistline.

"Please," her breathing is heavy, her brow furrowed, water and sweat trickling down her face and partially submerged bare chest.

I swallow again, knowing that I shouldn't but also that it will ease her pain if I help.

I place my hand over hers and gently guide her below the waistband of her compression shorts. I guide our hands, and with my hand still over hers, we start moving in a circular motion with just enough pressure to elicit a moaning gasp. Gray's brow furrows more as she presses into the motion of our fingers, her hips arching to increase the pressure. I can't take my eyes off her body as we find the right rhythm for what she needs. I'm drawn to her lips, where she's biting the bottom as the pleasure increases. Her other hand presses down on her lower abdomen.

"Hannah…" my name escapes her lips pleadingly as she climaxes.

Gray's body relaxes into the water as she's temporarily sated. Given the type of drugs used, I know that this is the first of many times we will do this tonight.

I reach up to touch her face and find that although it's still warm, it's not burning to the touch as before.

"Gray, Gray, can you open your eyes? Can you hear me?"

"Hannah?" She's sleepy and exhausted.

"Mmm, let's get you out of the tub and bed."

"The tub?" She struggles to open her eyes.

"It's okay. Just lean on me."

I managed to get her into a seated position in the tub. Her head rests on my shoulder as I reach around her hugging her closely as I begin to stand.

"Get your legs under you," I whisper. Gray nods into my shoulders, her arms wrapping around me as she struggles to regain footing.

"There we go. Big step up and out of the bath. Okay, let's get you out of these clothes."

I sit her on the toilet and begin to undress her. Unbuttoning the rest of her shirt, then moving to her pants.

"Wait…what's going on?" Gray still sounds drowsy but slightly more aware than before.

"It's okay. I'll get some other clothes if you want to undress."

Her eyes are open but she doesn't seem fully aware of what's happening.

"Can you undress? You need to get out of your wet clothes."

Gray nods, but when I stand up to leave, she clings to my hand, slumping forward.

"Shit. Kee!"

I knew Kee would be waiting outside the bedroom door even though I told them to leave. I'm thankful for her nosiness as I hear her entering the guest bedroom.

"What is it? What do you need?"

She glances at the corner and pulls up, seeing a half-naked Gray leaning against me.

"I need you to go to my room and grab some sweatpants and a shirt, please. I'll work on undressing Gray, and then I'll need your help getting her dressed. Okay?"

Kee nods and backs out of the room. I was expecting some type of ribbing from her. Still, I am glad that she understands the seriousness of the situation and keeps the jokes to herself.

"Gray, I will take your pants off, just your pants because they're soaking wet. I will then have Kee help get you dressed in some sweats and a shirt. Do you understand?"

She nods into my shoulder. "I don't…feel…right."

"I know, I know." I run my hand down the back of her head, pressing her into my shoulder and rubbing her back in a weak attempt at comforting her.

"Kiera gave you something, some drug. It will take a while to get it out of your system."

"Kiera?" It's a growl from the back of her throat, a sound I've never heard from her before. It makes the hair on the back of my neck stand up.

"Let's get you outta these wet clothes." She seems more aware now as she lifts her hips so I can slide her wet pants off.

"I'm back!" Kee calls from the room's doorway, giving me a heads-up before coming to the bathroom door.

"Thanks, Kee. Gray, I want you to lean on Kee while I dress you, okay?"

Nodding, Gray leans into me and lifts an arm for Kee to help her to her feet.

Between the two of us and Gray's feeble attempts to help, we get her dressed in a few minutes.

"Kee, let's get her to bed. She's fading fast." Gray's eyes flutter, and her head bobs as she tries to stay conscious.

"Thirsty," she manages through pale lips.

"Kee, can you run and get some water and maybe something light to snack on, like crackers, anything like that."

Nodding, Kee jogs from the room as I help Gray settle on the bed. I've pulled the cover and sheet aside so she can lie comfortably on the cool sheet.

"I need you to stay awake. I know you're tired, but you can't go to sleep just yet."

Kee returns with the water and some crackers from the kitchen.

"Thanks."

"Is Gray going to be alright?"

"I think so. We have to wait for the drugs to get out of her system. I'm hopeful it won't take too long, but we should plan for her to be here tomorrow just to be safe."

"Need anything else?"

"Do you mind grabbing me a change of clothes? My pajamas, if you could."

"You got it."

Handing me the glass of water and crackers, Kee heads back to my room, and I focus on Gray.

"Alright, sit up a little. There you go." I get a few sips of water in her as she fights the pull of the drugs back into unconsciousness.

I know it's only a matter of time before the drugs hit her again, and I want her to be settled and Kee to be back downstairs before that happens.

"Hannah…"

"I'm right here." Gently pushing the hair off her clammy forehead, the urge to kiss where my fingers just brushed is overwhelming.

"Where…where…am I?"

"You're at my place. It's safe here. I'll take care of you until you're better." Gray nods, finding my hand and holding it tightly as her breath hitches and becomes labored again.

"Here are your pajamas."

"Thanks, Kee. You can go now, and I mean it. I don't want you outside of the door. Do you understand?"

"Copy. I'll be in the kitchen if you need anything."

Shutting the door as she leaves, I turn back to Gray. Her skin is flushing again, starting in the middle of her chest, and working its way up her neck. It follows and spreads from her veins to her flesh, leaving its violent red trace behind.

"I…feel…"

"I know. It'll be over soon, I promise. Do you understand what's happening?"

"Yeah…yes." Gray moves our hands towards her waist.

"Do you want me to help you?"

Gray nods, giving her consent, and I let her move our hands to her core and hope this will be the last time.

CHAPTER 45

Gray

dreamt of her fingers on me. It had to have been a dream, right?

Fuck, my head hurts. No, my body hurts. Every inch of it, my skin feels itchy and hot.

It's hard to open my eyes. They're so heavy. I'm trying with all my strength and can barely get them to crack.

Where am I? What happened?

I can't remember much of last night other than being on the dancefloor with Kiera and being thirsty.

Fuck.

"Gray, can you hear me?"

Hannah's voice is like a bucket of ice-cold water splashing across me. I become fully conscious and manage to open my eyes.

A hiss escapes my lips at the light coming into the room from the window.

"Shoot, the window, sorry!" I can hear Hannah moving but can't seem to focus my eyes enough to track her.

I can't get my eyes to focus on anything. When I try to concentrate, everything spirals. It's like I drank too much and have the spins.

"I'm…going to throw up," I manage as I feel the burning bile rising in my throat.

Hannah is there immediately with a small trash can.

There's nothing in my body to expel except for the acidic bile. I spit once I'm done heaving and stay draped over the edge of the bed. This makes my head feel a bit better.

"Here, some water."

Hannah's feet disappear from my view as she passes me the glass of water, and I hear a faucet running not far away.

I barely have the strength to lift the glass to my lips but manage a few sips before setting it down heavily on the wood floor. I stay exactly as I am, waiting for my head to stop spinning and the world to make sense again.

Hannah's feet appear before me, and then a cool washcloth covers my neck. It's soothing, and I become drowsy almost immediately.

"Come on, let's get you back on the bed."

She gently places her hands on each of my shoulders and pushes me back, helping me sit in the bed. She adjusts the pillows to prop me up.

"Better now?" she asks as I lean back, letting the cool cloth soothe my pounding head.

"A little." My voice is raspy, and something tells me this isn't the first time I've thrown up since being here.

"What's going on?"

"I'll tell you in a bit once you're more awake and have recovered."

"Recovered? From what?" Even as I mumble the words, my head gets too heavy.

"Let's lay you back down. You need more sleep."

"Mmm." That is all I can manage as my body begins to shut down.

CHAPTER 46

Hannah

I t's the most coherent Gray's been since I brought her home. I'm exhausted. The night seemed to drag on forever, with Gray going from hot to cold, violently ill, and needing a release to settle.

I think the drugs are out of her system now, and the after-effects likely make Gray ill. The sun has been up for at least a few hours, and I know Kee and James probably wonder if everything is okay. I don't have the energy to go downstairs or even text them. I'm so tired.

Gray's soft breaths fill my ears, and I doze off as I sit beside her on the bed.

I might get some sleep since she seems to be getting better.

I crawl over Gray and lie down on the bed next to her. Tucking my body into hers and place my hand on her chest, I tell myself that it's so I can make sure she's okay, but I want to hold her too. No, I *need* to.

I feel sleep tugging at the corners of my brain.

CHAPTER 47

Gray

The weight of Hannah's hand on my chest is comforting as I climb out of whatever drugs still cling to my consciousness. I dreamt her hands were on me. No, I'm not dreaming. Her hands are on me.

Her hand is on my chest, her head on my shoulder, and one of her legs is thrown over mine.

She fits. Perfectly.

Pain hits me in the middle of my chest.

No, this is something else. I almost feel sad yet hopeful at the same time.

What is this? Fear? Love?

I don't want to move, but my stomach threatens to upend itself again, and I need to sit up or roll over something.

Shit.

Moving slowly, I slide her leg off before the need to vomit is too overwhelming for me to be coy about it.

I jerk upright and lean over the edge of the bed, vomiting into the trash can again. It's primarily dry heaving and a little bile at this point. My abs, no, my whole body hurts from the effort it takes to throw up.

Movement behind me tells me I've woken Hannah up. Still, before I apologize, a cool hand finds its way to my lower back, under my shirt, rubbing softly up and down.

"Okay?" Her voice is sleepy, soft, and full.

"Yeah, go back to sleep." My voice doesn't sound like my own. It's deeper, hoarse, and dark.

"Mmmm, we're up now. Let's get you some food and get you moving around a bit. You've been in this bed for almost twelve hours."

"What? What time is it or day is it?" I'm so confused. I hate it. I've never experienced anything like this before, the loss of time, the physical side effects, the overwhelming pain and desire that make my entire body thrum to the same rhythm of Hannah's strokes on my back.

Swallowing hard, I reach for the water and watch a shaking hand grab the glass of water. It doesn't feel like it belongs to me. Like my own limbs are not my own. Not controlled by me.

"I'll tell you everything once you've had some food. I've got soup downstairs. Let me go make it, and after you eat, we will get you to the sunroom to recover a bit more."

"I...I need to call Marcus."

"Later." Her voice has lost its sleepiness and has taken on a tone that I imagine she saves for patients at the hospital.

I can't bring myself to turn and look at her. There's a part of me that's deeply ashamed of my condition and something else just on the edge of my memory that keeps getting swallowed by the rolling fog of the drug.

"I'll be right back. Just sit back and take it easy for a few minutes, okay?"

I nod, still not looking at her.

What. The. Fuck. Happened.

I know in my gut that it has something to do with Kiera, and there are only so many reasons why my memory is fucked, and my body feels like this.

She drugged me.

"Kiera drugged me."

How could I have been so sloppy?

It must have been in the water she passed me when we stopped at the bar. I can't believe it. I shouldn't have let my guard down.

Sitting up, I slowly swing my legs over the edge of the bed. I'm in grey sweats and a white T-shirt that are definitely not mine, but they fit well enough, a bit tight, but they'll do. My body is still thrumming, pulsing from Hannah's touch, and I know that can only mean one thing. Given the type of drug Kiera likely dosed me with, I'm sure last night was quite interesting for Hannah.

"Fuck." I run my hand over my face. Everything feels hot and swollen still, even my hands. I know it's because my body is severely dehydrated, and I reach for the glass again.

"Get it together, Gray."

Taking a few sips, I take in the rest of the room. My clothes hang from a few different doorknobs and are drying out.

Why…would they be wet?

A part of me wants to know, and the other part, full of shame, doesn't want to know anything about what happened, how it happened, and who it happened with.

The shame almost makes me heave again, but I manage to hold down the water I just drank.

As I run my hand over my face, I hear Hannah in the hallway. For a moment, I consider trying to sit up straight to appear like I'm feeling better, but it won't happen. I can barely stay sitting on the end of the bed. Given what she had to deal with throughout the night, I likely had nothing to hide from her. She's probably seen and heard everything.

"I hope chicken noodle soup is okay. It's all I had in the pantry."

"My favorite." My voice is more of a croak, and I wince as my vocal cords rasp against each other. Taking another sip of water, I take the soup from her. She takes the trash can from my feet and disappears into the bathroom.

Smelling the soup makes my stomach turn, but I know I need

to eat something. Trying not to breathe in its smell, I take a small sip of the broth, waiting for it to come back up.

I wait for another bite until Hannah returns, just in case I need the trash can again.

"Is it alright?"

Nodding, I look at her for the first time since waking up.

Jesus, she's stunning. Even with circles under her eyes, her hair in a sloppy pony, and dressed in baggy pajamas, she's…

"Beautiful."

"What?" she chuckles slightly, looking like I've gone crazy.

"What? Oh, um, the soup it's beautiful." Clearing my throat, I force another spoonful down, chasing it with more water.

"Don't eat too much or too fast. Your body is still recovering." She's pushing the hair off my forehead as if it's something we've always done, as if we've known each other for longer than we have. The familiarity of it clears some of the drug fog.

"I'm…I'm sorry about…everything. You had to…um…help me with…uh…certain things." I feel the heat rising, and my cheeks are flaming before the sentence is even out of my mouth.

"You remember! I didn't think you would have much memory of what happened last night."

"I'm still piecing everything together, but I assume Kiera drugged me. Unfortunately, I'm familiar with the drugs she likes to play with, so I can imagine how the night went. I'm sorry you had to deal with that. But I appreciate everything you've done for me."

Hannah looks at me strangely. "I don't think I've ever seen you like this before. You don't have any reason to be embarrassed or ashamed. Someone did this to you against your will. You didn't have a choice in the matter."

It's hard for me to hear it from someone else, and my throat tightens. I'm not good with vulnerability, and I start to close myself off, so I don't have to address it.

"Right." I force a small, thin-lipped smile and glance in her direction. "I appreciate it either way, and I am sorry that you got caught up in this."

"What exactly is 'this,' Gray? Who is Kiera, and why did she do this?"

Tilting my head back, I close my eyes and take a deep breath.

"When I started working for Dimitri, he would assign me to be his daughter's bodyguard. Kiera is his daughter, and when I started acting as her bodyguard, things got a bit blurry between us. We dated for a while, and the breakup was messy. Her dad got involved, and let's just say I learned a valuable and painful lesson on shitting where you eat."

I'm uncomfortable and need to move, but I can't stand, so I scratch the back of my neck instead.

"Since we broke up, I haven't dealt with her too often, but I'm assigned to her whenever she's in town. My job is to do whatever she wants, and if I don't, there's punishment involved. She's never done anything like this before, though. There's always flirting and dancing, but nothing like this. She took it too far this time."

"How long were the two of you together?" Hannah's voice is soft, strained.

"Nine months." I glance at her and can see that she's surprised at the length of time we have been together.

"I see, and there's nothing there now, nothing between you two?" Her arms are crossed. Now she's the one shutting down.

"Nothing, I swear. Like I said, she's possessive, always has been, and always flirting, but there's nothing there on my end. There hasn't been in a long time."

"How long ago did you date?"

"It's been a few months since we ended things."

The silence is palpable between us, and I take another spoonful of the now-cold chicken noodle soup.

"Why did she drug you?"

"I've been thinking about it, and it may be because she saw us in the club together the other night. When we were dancing. She knows I don't dance or do stuff like that, so she likely assumed that we were together, and this was her way of…proving a point, I guess."

"What are you going to do? We should report it to the police."

"I can't do that. I can't do anything about it. Dimitri, let's just say it won't end well for me if I go to the authorities or address it with her."

"Who is this Dimitri guy, and what exactly do you mean by punishment? What the fuck is going on in that club, Gray?"

I look at her, and every fiber of my being wants to confide in her. I want to tell her everything. I want to tell her how I got the scar on my face, but I can't. The tightening in my throat gets worse, and swallowing takes effort around the lump forming there.

Guilt, shame, I hate that I can't share this part of my life with her.

I look away, unable to lie to her. I can't look her in the face and tell her everything will be fine, that the club is exactly what it seems. That nothing is going on there, that everything will be fine. I can't lie to her, but I know I have to.

Forcing the lump down in my throat, I swallow all my guilt and shame, forcing them to the pit of my stomach where they sit and sour.

"It's nothing, I'll just get my hours cut or something at the club, and I need the work. Dimitri has done so much for me that I could never go to the authorities over this." I try to force a smile, but it's more grimace. The words sound hollow even as I say them.

"You're a shit liar, Gray," Hannah mutters as she abruptly leaves the room.

Fuck.

CHAPTER 48

Hannah

I don't know why Gray is lying to me. She almost overdosed from whatever that woman gave her. Maybe Kiera means more to Gray than she's letting on, so she doesn't want to turn her in. I don't understand why Gray wouldn't want to do anything about this.

She could have died.

My heart clenches at the thought, and I lean against the wall in the hallway, trying to catch my breath.

I can't seem to steady myself; tears are burning at the corners of my eyes, threatening to spill over, and I can't stop them from falling.

"Hannah…" Her voice is soft and lingers in the air between us as I struggle to stifle the sobs breaking loose. "I'm fine, I promise." Gray's arms wrap around me from behind. Gently curling me into her body which still seems too warm.

"But you almost weren't. You could have easily died if she had given you more. Do you understand that?" Turning, I rest my head on Gray's chest, pulling her closer.

"I understand. I know it was scary. I was scared too. I'm pissed at Kiera for doing this to me, to us, and I will address it with her. But I need you to understand that many different things are at play here.

She's the boss' daughter. Not to mention stirring the pot at work is one of the worst things you can do."

"Can't you just quit?"

"I wish I could, but there are…things…about that place that you don't understand, and I can't tell you about them, so I need you to trust me. I will leave Midnight. I just can't do it yet."

Pressing my face into her chest, I nod and decide to believe what Gray says. I'll trust her and hope she can eventually tell me what is happening at Midnight.

CHAPTER 49

Gray

"Jesus Christ, Gray. You alright?"

"Hey Marcus, thanks, man. Thanks for what you did. I'm sorry. I know that it probably put you in a tough spot."

Marcus comes in for a hug then, holding me by the shoulders, gives me the once over.

"You sure you're okay to work tonight?"

"Yeah, I don't want to cause any issues with Dimitri, so I figure it's best not to skip out on more shifts."

"Well, his fucking daughter tried to drug and rape you, so I think that gets you a couple of days off."

Hearing the words sends a shiver through my body, echoing in my brain. It will take a while for what happened to sink in fully, but Marcus voicing them makes everything seem more real.

We look at each other, Marcus giving me a gentle smile and a pat on the shoulder.

"I'm glad you're back either way. It hasn't been the same without you here. How's Hannah, by the way? Is she okay? How's she dealing with all of this?"

"Honestly, not great. She's shaken up, which is understandable.

She wanted to go to the authorities." Marcus' head snaps up as soon as I mention the cops.

"Don't worry, I managed to talk her out of it, but she's scared and angry and doesn't understand why I can't do anything about what happened."

"What are you going to do?"

"I mean… I guess I'll talk to Kiera about it, I'm sure she knows what she did was wrong, but I'll need to sit down and explain why and let her know it wasn't okay. Does Dimitri know about it?"

Scratching the back of his neck and avoiding my eyes, he spills the news to me, "I had to tell him why you disappeared and why you weren't in the next day. I didn't have a choice, and I think Kiera may have already told him what she'd done. He didn't seem surprised."

Fuck.

"Great." My stomach flips, thinking about what punishment he might have for me. "Do you think he'll do anything about it to either of us?"

"I have no idea. If I were you, I'd lay as low as possible tonight and keep your head down. You understand?"

"Yeah, I got you. Thanks for covering for me and saving my ass the other night."

"No worries, I always got your back, kid."

Marcus wanders off to chat with the crew as I head to the bar to get a water bottle. I'm still dealing with the side effects of the drug and am extremely thirsty and dehydrated. The headache haunting me for the last several days still lingers behind my eyes, and I can't seem to get rid of it no matter how many pills I take.

My body feels unsteady, off-balance like I'm not fully controlling it. It's been several days since I was drugged, but it still lingers.

I can't help but glance up at Dimitri's office as I take a swig of water, ensuring it's from a sealed bottle. The lights are off, maybe I'll get lucky, and he won't come in tonight. Possibly Kiera will be absent as well.

I don't know how to address this with Kiera, but I can't let this go. She endangered my life, affecting Hannah and me, and I won't stand for that. Hannah's been acting differently towards me since that night, and I can only imagine what she went through.

Sometimes, it seems like she's too embarrassed to look at my face and doesn't want to be close to me anymore. Given what Kiera is willing to do, she's backing away, maybe for the best.

CHAPTER 50

Hannah

I don't know when or how my feelings changed, but they did. I was so worried. I want Gray with all my being, and now there is something else there, something different. I still want her, but I want more than just the physical aspects of her. I need more, and I'm unsure how to explain it to Gray. Seeing Gray hurt and drugged by Kiera made me realize how important Gray is to me.

It's weird how it works, but I want her more now than I did before, but I find myself pulling back. What happened to Gray was crazy and terrifying. I can't help but wonder if stuff like that happens all the time. If she's got crazy ex-girlfriends who also happen to be her boss' daughter willing to drug and assault her, who else does she have lurking around?

I have enough to worry about with my dad's case and my safety. Maybe we should call it quits before it gets too severe. End it before we become too attached to each other. That way, it's easier to part ways.

But what if it's already too late for that?

CHAPTER 51

Gray

"Gray, the boss is looking for you." Luke's voice rings through my earpiece, bringing my worst fears to light. I feel my stomach drop. He would want to talk with me about only one thing, and there's no telling which direction this conversation will go.

As I walk towards the stairs leading up to Dimitri's office, I see Marcus walking towards me out of my peripheral vision.

"Everything will be fine, kid. Just bite your tongue, don't talk back, and agree with whatever he says. Okay?" He's gripping my shoulder as he walks with me towards the stairs.

None of us like being called into Dimitri's office, least of all me. The last time I went in there, I walked out with a cut slicing down the left side of my face. I prepare myself mentally as I walk up the stairs. I can feel the eyes of the others on me as I slowly work my way to Dimitri's office.

I'm in no rush to get to his office, but I know that if I take too long, it will irritate him and make him lash out even more. I can handle this. I need to be ready to take whatever he will dish out when I go there.

Standing outside Dimitri's office, my heart races, and I can feel the panic building. I can feel the blade running down my face all over again. The sting, the overwhelming sense of helplessness, and the pain rush back as I reach for the door handle. Taking a deep, steadying breath, I step inside.

CHAPTER 52

Hannah

"Gray was supposed to be here an hour ago, and I haven't heard anything from her. Should I be worried?"

"I'm sure Gray is fine. I bet it was a long night last night at the club, and she's just sleeping in. Give Gray some time to wake up and get moving before you worry too much. It's still early."

I know Kee is trying to reassure me, but Gray said she would be here at nine am, and it's already past ten making me think that something terrible has happened. I highly doubt that Gray is sleeping in this late anyway.

"I don't know. I have a bad feeling. I'm worried something's happened. This was Gray's first night back after the incident with Kiera. What if Dimitri or Kiera did something to Gray?"

Kee pauses. "Listen, I did some digging on Kiera and Dimitri, and it isn't good. There are a lot of rumors about that family. The local authorities say they are Russian mafia and do a lot of importing of drugs and weapons. The nightclub is a front to help launder money." Taking a breath Kee looks down at her hands. "Hannah, there's no easy way to say this, but I don't think Gray is who you think she is, and if she's involved with Dimitri and Kiera, you may want to walk away from all of this before it gets more complicated."

"I appreciated what you're saying, Kee, but I trust Gray, and I know she wouldn't do anything to hurt me. Why can't you and James get on board with this?"

"We're your bodyguards first, Hannah. Friends second."

Kee's words are like a slap to the face. I step back and square my shoulders, determined not to back down or cry.

"I'm going to see if Gray is okay. Are you coming with me or not?"

"Listen, let's give Gray another hour, and if she doesn't call or show up James or I can run over to their place to check in on them. How does that sound?"

"I want to go too."

"Absolutely not. If something has happened to Gray, the last thing we need is to put you in danger. You'll stay here while one of us checks it out. That's final. No negotiating."

I nod, even though I'm not happy with this.

I recheck my phone, willing for Gray to call or text me.

CHAPTER 53

Gray

"So, I heard you and my daughter had a bit of a run-in the other night." Dimitri's voice is cold and emotionless, slicing through the air like a sharpened knife.

I give a slight nod in response. I'm not sure my voice is steady enough to speak. Looking around the room, I notice that we are not alone. There are three guards in the room with us. None of whom I know. Dimitri's special guards and henchmen do all of his nefarious bidding.

"I hope you understand that she regrets her actions and recognizes her wrongdoings in approaching the situation."

I nod again, biting the inside of my cheek to wrangle my fear, anxiety, and anger. I can taste blood.

"Am I right in assuming that there are no hard feelings and that I don't need to worry about you doing anything stupid in retaliation?"

A nod.

"Now, I want to discuss this woman you've been seeing."

I freeze.

"My understanding is that she's the daughter of D.A. Winters. Is that correct?"

I don't move.

Dimitri nods to one of the guards. I see him move out of the corner of my eye and start to turn but not fast enough. His fist catches the right side of my face, snapping my head around to the left and making my teeth catch the inside of my cheek, ripping it open with the corner of my mouth.

I stumble to the left, caught by one of the other guards, and stood in front of Dimitri's desk.

"She's the daughter of D.A. Winters, is that correct?"

A nod. Blood runs from my mouth as it fills from the cut on my cheek.

"She's not to come into this club again. You're to stay close to her and report to me on her weekly movements. Do you understand?"

I'm still processing what he's said when the second blow to the right side of my face drops me to my knees.

On my hands and knees, I shake my head to clear the fog quickly, hoping to evade other blows. I spit blood on the floor as I struggle to my feet.

"Do. You. Understand?" Dimitri leans forward, a knife gleaming in his hand. The same knife he used on my face a few months ago.

I swallow hard, coating my mouth in blood.

I nod again, feeling my heart drop to the pit of my stomach.

"I want to know who she's seeing, what she's doing, and if she knows anything about her father's investigation. You'll be my eyes and ears, and if I don't like the effort you're putting in, I'll send someone more adept than Roy to scare her."

Fuck, Roy. I had forgotten about Roy.

"I really have to thank you for this idea. Roy was more than willing to share how you worked behind the scenes for me." Dimitri's smile is chilling.

"I'll put this plainly for you, Gray. If you mess this up, I'll not only come for you but also make sure that the lovely Hannah is punished, and I'll let you watch." He smiles again and nods to his men.

They each grab an arm and haul me out of the office, pushing me onto the walkway above the club.

I know Marcus is likely watching me, and I try to keep my shit together, but it's too much, and panic starts to take over. My body starts to shake, and I turn to the guard locker room, but I'm unsure if I can make my legs work. I'm holding onto the railing for dear life when I feel someone grab my arm.

"Come on, kid, not here."

Marcus.

CHAPTER 54

Hannah

I t's been two hours, and I still haven't heard from Gray. I'm officially worried now and am sure that something must have happened. Gray always responds to my texts and calls, and not hearing anything from them makes my stomach knot.

"Kee, I want you or James to go and check on Gray, please. I can't stop worrying about them."

Nodding, Kee radios James, who is out front in the car.

"James will go to Gray's and check on things."

I grip the phone, hoping that everything is alright.

CHAPTER 55

Gray

My place is quiet, and nothing seems out of place for 11 AM on a Sunday. Everyone is probably having a nice slow morning, and here I am, lying in bed with a woman who isn't Hannah.

I feel sick to my stomach. I can't believe I'm doing this.

A knock on the door, and I hear James calling my name. He's impatient and is knocking again before I can leave the bed. The woman in my bed stirs, rolling over before rising with me and shuffling to the restroom.

I walk to the door shirtless and disheveled. I need to make this look good.

"James? What…uh…what are you doing here?" I glance behind me and move my head to my bedmate, so she stays out of James' eye line.

"I could ask you the same fucking question, Gray." James pushes the door open, knocking me back several paces.

"You've got to be kidding me. You son-of-a-bitch!" James' fist connects with my already bruised right cheek sending me sprawling on the floor.

My "guest" is a young woman desperately trying to get dressed in the corner.

"What the fuck, man?" I slur from the floor.

"Hannah has been calling and texting you all morning, you were supposed to meet her at nine this morning, and she's been worried something happened to you since you never showed up. I guess you were too 'busy' with your friend here to check your fucking phone."

I close my eyes briefly before looking at James, giving him a lop-sided smirk and shrugging my shoulders, acting as if he didn't just catch me cheating on Hannah.

"You, get your shit and get out. And you, don't bother coming by the house or contacting Hannah again."

James moves aside for the woman as she flees from the room, and he then slams the door. Leaving me alone on the floor of my apartment.

Well, that couldn't have gone any better. I could've done without the punch, but it was warranted. I deserve it, and it makes everything seem more real.

I hoped she would send James or Kee over if I didn't show up. It was a gamble, but it's paid off. I need her to think I'm a terrible person, that I don't care for her.

Still sitting on my floor, I rub my swollen and sore face with my hands, willing the tears away. I haven't cried in a long time, and the feeling of tears prickling the corners of my eyes is unsettling.

I feel a hollowness opening in my chest at the thought that I've ruined everything with Hannah.

I deserve everything I get from here on out. I'm disgusted with myself and hope that when this is all over, Hannah will be able to forgive me and see that what I did was to keep her safe.

I'm guilty, but I know what I did was the best thing for Hannah. It's better if she's not in my life. It's safer for her if she's not around me. There were probably better ways to do this, but I needed her to be mad. I need her to hate me.

I can't have her coming into Midnight anymore. It's too big of a risk. It's best to keep her as far from me as possible.

I'll let Dimitri know that Hannah and I had a falling out. I'm no longer able to get close to her, and hopefully, that will buy me some time to figure out what the fuck I'm going to do.

How do I get us both out of this in one piece?

CHAPTER 56

Hannah

"What do you mean she was with someone else? Like, she had a guest or a friend over?"

"No, she was *with* someone."

James' voice fades, and a buzzing fills my ears.

She was with someone. What the fuck is going on?

"I…I…need a minute." Walking away from James and Kee, I can feel the heat creeping up my face. I'm such an idiot. How could I think someone like Gray would be happy with someone like me? There's no way I could give her everything she needs to be satisfied. My life is a mess; no one would want to deal with all of this anyway. I can't really blame Gray for trying to get out of this.

Still, it fucking hurts. *I* hurt. There's already an emptiness forming where Gray once was.

I knew this would happen, and I still moved forward and fell for Gray.

I'm such an idiot.

Picking up my phone, I dial Gray's number. She doesn't answer the first time or the second, but the third time I hit "send" she answers on the second ring.

"What's going on? Why are you doing this?" I can barely keep the shaking out of my voice, but I'm determined to stay strong.

"Listen, being with you was a mistake. You don't fit in my world. You were just a hookup anyway, something to entertain me for a moment." Gray's voice is dull, utterly devoid of any emotion. It's not like her.

"I don't understand this."

"There isn't anything to understand, Hannah. You were a fun time. I was bored, that's it. Don't bother me at work anymore."

I swear Gray's voice wavers momentarily before becoming cold and steeled again.

"Gray, please, I need you to explain…" The line goes dead. Gray hung up on me! I immediately call her again, only to have the call go to voicemail.

"What is going on?" I wonder out loud. Turning to look at James and Kee as if they could offer some clarity, I catch them whispering to themselves.

"What are you two talking about? What's going on?" I walk towards the living room fighting the sinking feeling in my stomach with every step.

"Maybe you should call Cassie?" Kee offers with a sympathetic smile.

"I'm not calling anyone. What were you two talking about? Spill it." Looking from James to Kee, I see a look pass between them.

"I was just telling Kee that this isn't that big of a surprise to me. Gray is involved in some bad shit, Hannah. It was only a matter of time before she did something like this." James crosses his arms over his chest as he finishes talking. Kee won't look me in the eyes but instead seems to study her shoes intensely.

"I don't believe you, James, and I don't believe Gray. I will figure out whatever is happening here, so you might as well tell me."

"I'm sorry, Hannah, but there's nothing to tell you. We're not lying," Kee says, looking at me.

The tears I've been fighting finally win and streak down my

face. Confused, hurt, and feeling betrayed, I turn and head to the sunroom.

Closing the double doors behind me, I curl up on the sofa and let the sun soothe my troubled mind.

* * *

"Tell me what you're thinking about." James' voice cuts through the fog that I've lost myself in.

"Honestly, I wasn't really thinking about anything."

I haven't had much appetite over the last week since falling out with Gray, and I can't seem to eat this meal either.

James and Kee are across from me, watching me play with my food. I know they're worried about me, but I can't get over how easy it was for Gray to just toss me aside.

I've called Gray several times only to be sent directly to voicemail. I can't bring myself to leave a message. I tell myself I'm not that pathetic and don't miss her much. But the truth is that I'm falling to pieces, and Gray simply moved on as if nothing had happened between us, like what we had hadn't felt permanent, like we were meant to be together.

Had it all been in my head?

Had Gray played me the entire time?

I can't bring myself to believe that. Something else has to be going on. I need to talk to Gray and see them for myself. I need to look Gray in the eyes and hear them say it's over between us.

I hit send on my phone and watch as the message pops up in my conversation with Cassie.

> Cassie: What do Kee and James think about this?
> Me: They don't need to know. I'm going to sneak out, and I'll meet you at the park.
> Cassie: Are you sure about this, Hannah? Is Gray worth this? Worth risking your life?
> Me: Yes, now are you in or not?
> Cassie: I'm in. Text me when you're on your way to the park.

Confidence settles into my bones. I know it's stupid and dangerous, but I don't know what else to do, and right now, I don't feel like I can trust James and Kee.

"I'm going to bed early tonight." I push my plate away from me and get up from the kitchen table.

They rise from the table, and concern flashes across Kee's face, "Are you feeling okay? It's pretty early. Do you want anything else to eat?"

"I'm good." My short response puts an end to any other conversation.

Leaving them in the kitchen, I walk up to my room and immediately turn out the lights, hoping that James, Kee, and the other security guards will see this and lower their guard.

They're looking for people sneaking in, not out, and I'm hoping that will work in my favor.

I put on a pair of skintight black jeans, boots, and a low-cut black silk shirt, putting my black coat on. Now I just need to wait until James and Kee settle in for the night.

CHAPTER 57

Gray

I t's like any other night at Midnight's. It's packed with undulating bodies, the smell of liquor and sweat drifting up from the dance-floor. I told Dimitri about Hannah and me yesterday. I received an excellent new blackened eye for it and a reminder that if I don't put in an honest effort, I won't be the only one being punished.

I have no idea what I'm going to do. I can't have Hannah involved in this, and I can't say "no" to Dimitri for fear of what he might do to her. How do I spin this to make it work? How can I…

My brain stops working, and all thoughts cease.

Hannah.

I can't take my eyes off her as she weaves through the dancefloor to the bar. I could pick her out of any crowd, but she looks beyond stunning tonight. Her low-cut silk shirt and skin-tight jeans fit her body perfectly, and her strawberry-blonde hair is pulled up in a sloppy ponytail, my favorite. Her pale skin seems to glow as she leans over the bar to ask for a drink.

Fuck me.

I look away long enough to notice that Dimitri is standing on the platform above me, watching me, watching Hannah.

I have to get her out of here. I need her to be as far away from

Dimitri as possible. I don't know if she'll even talk to me, let alone listen to anything I have to say, but I have to try.

Taking a breath, I start down the stairs and head towards Hannah and her friend Cassie.

CHAPTER 58

Hannah

haven't snuck out of a house in over a decade, and the tingling of excitement in my stomach is mixed with the nervousness of getting caught.

I slip out of my room, boots in hand. I know James is in the car, and Kee is in the guest room downstairs or the living room. It's early enough that she should still be in the living room. Which means I can sneak out through the sunroom and take the narrow alley between the townhomes to the next block over. From there, I can easily job to the park and meet Cassie.

It's simple. I can do this.

My house is old, and the stairs creak as I painstakingly work my way down them. My sock-clad feet barely touch the wood to silence my betraying house. I make it down the stairs and pause, listening for Kee.

All I can hear is my hushed breathing and heart beating. I swear she can probably hear it from the other room.

I look down the hall and don't see any lights on in the guest room. She's either asleep or still sitting in the living room. Turning, I glance quickly towards the living room, where I can see the low dim light of a lamp.

Good.

I start down the hall towards the sunroom. Carefully placing each of my steps to avoid the squeaky boards. The sunroom floor is tile and cold against my feet. I pause briefly to put my boots on and then slip silently through the back door. I have no idea where the other security guards are, but I'm not stopping for anyone. I open the wooden fence gate and slip into the alley. I stay low, crouching like I've seen them do in the movies. Trying to stay small and in the shadows.

Not seeing or hearing anything, I head down the alley and break out onto the next street.

Cassie sends a thumbs-up, and I start jogging down the street. The park is only two blocks away, and I can make quick work of those.

Arriving at the park, I stand in the shadow of the gate until I see a pair of headlights. Stepping out, I try to see if the car is Cassie; waving at the car, it slows, stopping.

Thank God it's Cassie.

"You ready to get your woman back?" She asks, rolling the window down and smiling at me.

"Let's do this!" I say, exhilarated and feeling confident given that I've just given my security the slip.

Less than fifteen minutes later, we're walking into Club Midnight. Luke gives us a tight smile and directs us to the coat check, and Cassie and I head towards the bar. Letting the music and the bodies carry us towards our destination.

Leaning over the bar, Cassie leans over and whispers into my ear, "Heads up, Gray is heading this way." I look past Cassie and can see her dark figure moving swiftly through the crowd towards us. She looks pissed…and there's something else there that I can't quite place.

Gray looks tired and thin and has a nasty black eye. She was hit hard enough that the blood vessels around her pupil burst, leaving her vision bloodied.

What happened? I know I shouldn't care, but I can't stop myself from being concerned for Gray.

Gray walks up, looking from me to Cassie before turning back to me.

"You need to leave."

Gray's words hit me like a slap in the face.

"What?"

"You need to leave. You can't be here." Gray's voice is devoid of any and all emotion. It's almost harsh.

Before I can say anything, Cassie jumps in, "Don't tell her where she can and can't be. You don't own this place. She can be here if she wants!"

While I appreciate Cassie jumping in to defend me, this isn't worth my time or effort. Gray, who I thought was worth it, just proved that she isn't. Is it stupid to give up so easily?

"You don't understand what I'm saying. You can't be here." Gray moves their head slightly as if gesturing to something.

I follow and look up to see that we are all being watched by a man dressed from head to toe in black.

"Who is that?"

"Dimitri, he's the owner. He's requested that you not be a patron at the bar."

"Whose fault is that?" Cassie snarls.

"Mine, I'm sure, but it's for the best, I promise."

"Why should we listen to anything you say? You've proven you're nothing more than a liar and a cheat." Cassie, beside me, moves closer to Gray with every word as if she's going to push Gray.

"That's enough. You're causing a scene. Let's just go. I don't want to be here anyway." I make sure to look directly at Gray with my last words. This is me letting go. "There's nothing here for me."

I know my words have hit their mark as Gray's eyes flicker. It's all the closure I will get; for now, that's fine. I do have questions, and Gray will answer them, just not here, not at Midnight.

"I'd like to go, please." My voice cracks as I fight back the tears burning at the corners of my eyes.

"Pig," Cassie says, turning and grabbing my arm to lead me out of the club, but not before giving Gray another glare and snarl.

Every step away from Gray, I feel a piece of myself turning colder and colder, shutting down and turning inward.

I look back again, hoping Gray will follow behind or look after us as we walk away. But she isn't. She's already turned and returned to her post on the platform under the watchful eye of the man in black.

The vision of Gray walking away from me will haunt me like a ghost.

I hang my head and let the tears fall as Cassie ushers me through the doors of Midnight and back to reality.

CHAPTER 59

Gray

My chest hurts. Deep in my chest, it's getting worse with every breath I take as I try to calm myself.

I want to run after her, I want to hold her, I want to wipe her tears away. Tears that I've caused. I want to apologize again and again until my voice is hoarse. I need her so badly with every fiber of my being. She's like water, I need her to survive, and I just made her walk away.

The look on her face will be seared in my brain forever.

I can feel the panic building and try calming my breathing, but it worsens. I need to get out of here. I need to get away. I scan the crowd for Marcus.

I reach for my earpiece to radio Marcus, but a hand grabs my arm before I can key in.

One of Dimitri's men stands over me, and his grip tightens on my arm.

"Dimitri wants to see you."

I nod, my throat closing as the panic builds. As I follow the guard up the stairs, I glance around for Marcus again.

I know I will be punished, and I'm tempted to run. What if I just cut out and disappeared? What would happen? Would they find me? Would they go after Hannah? Would Dimitri go after those he could find if I disappeared? What about Marcus?

I can barely breathe as I step into the office. It's cold and dark. There are four guards and Dimitri all standing as I walk in.

The guard behind me pushes me forward, so I'm in the middle of the room. Surrounded.

"I thought I told you to never have her come to this club again?"

"I told her I didn't think she would come here. I thought I had made it clear, I…I didn't know she was coming."

"I don't know if I believe you." A nod. A punch.

"Why was she here."

I try to catch my breath. "I don't know, they just came." A nod. A punch.

On my knees, spitting blood and gasping. I know where this is going and brace myself for the onslaught of hits and kicks.

"You're not very convincing, Gray." A nod.

The group closes in on me. I manage to defend against a few hits, but soon I'm on my side, curling in, trying to protect my head and ribs as much as I can against the blows.

I'm losing consciousness as pain in my side starts. It feels like knives, and I know I've broken ribs.

"Dump her near the girl's place. I want to send a message."

With another blow, my vision starts to close in before fading to black.

CHAPTER 60

Hannah

Cassie drops me off a block from my house after taking me to our favorite late-night drive-thru for a quick snack.

I don't even care if I get caught now as I walk down my street. I have my answer and am still fuming over what Gray said. Yet, when I see the headlights coming my way, something tells me to hide. I learned long ago to listen to my instincts; this instance is no different.

Seeing the headlights heading in my direction, I duck behind the stairs of a townhouse about four down from where I live. I can see James sitting in the car across the street.

I hold my breath as the vehicle slows, illuminating James briefly before he ducks out of sight.

The car stops two doors away from me, between where I'm hiding and the safety of James and my home.

A car door opens, and several figures emerge. I can make them out in the dim light of the lone streetlamp as they appear to grab something and dump it next to the steps of the townhome two houses down.

The car drives away slowly, and I sink farther into the shadows. I hear James opening the car door and watch as he investigates.

Do I stay here, or do I go see it as well? I don't like this at all.

I slowly look around to ensure that the street is empty before I step out from next to the steps and walk down the block to a dark lump on the ground.

"James?" I call quietly as he crosses the street towards me.

"Hannah, what the fuck are you doing out here. Don't take another step. I need to see what this is, and then we'll have a fucking heart-to-heart about what you think you're doing."

I don't know what to say. I've never heard or seen James so angry, so I stop and let him approach the pile next to the stairs.

"Fuck!"

I'm moving as soon as I hear his exclamation.

"Hannah! Hannah, stop, stay there!"

"What is it?!" I can't stop myself, and I'm suddenly filled with panic and dread as I get close enough to see the look on James' face.

I follow his stricken eyes, and everything stops.

It's Gray, and she's in a bad way. Gray is pale, shockingly so, and doesn't seem conscious. All I can see is the blood on her face and the bruises covering her arms. It's too much blood.

From somewhere near me, I hear James speak into the radio, "Kee, meet me at the front of the house, now!"

"Why?"

"Now, Kee!"

I reach for Gray, but James grabs her, slinging an arm over his shoulder, lifting her up as gently as possible, and starting towards the townhouse. Snapping out of it, I rush forward, grabbing Gray's other arm and putting it over my shoulder, mimicking James.

As we climb the stairs, Kee opens the door, "What the fuck is going on! Hannah, what are you doing out?"

"I don't know. Some thugs dumped Gray a couple of houses down. I need you to go grab the medkit. Hurry!"

Kee runs off as we lay Gray's limp, cold body on the kitchen table.

I step back and look at Gray on the kitchen table, and my heart stops. My world is torn asunder by the scene in the kitchen.

Gray's lifeless body on the table, James giving her CPR, and Kee dialing the phone frantically as she drops the medical kit by my feet.

"No pulse." James is breathless, and I can see the sweat forming on his brow from the exertion of trying to revive Gray. "CPR doesn't seem to be working."

I let my training take over and switched with James to give him a break. Checking for a pulse before resuming compressions, there's a brief moment of panic when I don't feel anything.

"Okay, that's okay." I'm trying to remain calm while I'm screaming and terrified on the inside.

"Kee, what are they saying?"

"The ambulance will be here less than five minutes from your hospital, so they're close."

"Good, that's good. Tell them we'll need an epi, and they'll need to be ready to take over CPR and have the defibrillator ready."

"Copy." I focus on breathing and listen as Kee relays my message to the dispatch.

"Ambo is here," James calls, and from the corner of my eye, I see the lights reflecting through the house.

"Let them in, and hurry, please." I'm getting tired, and Gray has been down for too long. We need to get a heartbeat and administer a shock immediately.

I know the paramedics from the hospital, and we immediately fall into our routine, with one of them taking over compressions while the other bags. I step back to let them work and try to steady my breathing.

I can look at Gray's body fully for the first time and in the light.

There are bruises everywhere, with a large portion of her ribs covered. Gray probably has broken ribs, maybe a perforated lung. Who knows what internal injuries she might have.

"Alright, we've got a pulse. Let's move!"

I must have spaced out or something because we were suddenly moving towards the ambulance, and Gray was breathing on her own.

As we get into the ambulance, Kee gets in with us, and James tells me he'll meet us there.

Gray isn't awake, and she is struggling to breathe.

"How are her lungs?" I ask, trying not to step on toes, but at the same time, the concern I feel is overwhelming and driving me mad.

"Shallow breaths on the right side, probably a punctured lung." I nod as they verify what I already know.

Reaching out, I grab Gray's hand and hold it tight. It's cold but warms under my hand the longer I have it.

Gray's eyes flutter briefly as if she's trying to open them but is unsuccessful. I can see the bruises still forming across Gray's face and the lacerations that the medics are trying to stem the flow of, and yet I feel like I'm not seeing anything. It's like time has slowed, sound has disappeared, and I can only focus on Gray's hand in mine.

I focus on the feeling of her fingers warming under my hand. The roughness of her skin against the smoothness of mine.

Focus on a tiny thing, and the rest will be fine. I know it's not true, but it's all I can do now to keep myself together.

Everything will be fine.

CHAPTER 61

Gray

Pain leaks into my consciousness. The pain starts in my chest, radiating out to my side, ribs, hands, head, and body. I've not felt pain like this before and have lost all sense of time and place. This means I've likely been unconscious for a while. As I slowly note my body, I let my consciousness float forward and open my eyes.

I'm in a hospital. I can hear the beeping of the machines, my machines.

How bad is it?

The last thing I remember was being in Dimitri's office and getting knocked around. It went too far this time. It must have if I've ended up here.

My body is cold, except for my left hand, which seems to be on fire. It's so warm. I turn my head, wincing as pain laces from behind my eyes, through my neck, and into my lower back.

Hannah. She's here. Holding my hand while she sleeps. She looks exhausted even as she sleeps, with dark circles under her eyes and her hair in a sloppy bun. She's in her scrubs.

I use what little strength I can muster to squeeze her hand.

She wakes up immediately and looks up at me.

"You're awake!"

"Hey…" At least that's what I try to say, but my voice is so hoarse it's more of a croak and a cough.

"Water… You need some water. Your throat will be sore for a while from being intubated."

Intubated? Jesus, what happened?

"Here, you go, just a few small sips."

"Wha…what happened?" I manage to grunt out as I attempt to sit up.

"Don't get up yet. You need to recover more before you try to move around. You were dumped in front of my home by Dimitri's men. James saw them do it and got you into the house before you were too far gone. We had to do CPR on you for quite a while before you returned to us."

"When we got you to the hospital, they had to intubate and put a chest tube on the left side. You're lucky to be alive."

I can't seem to form the words to thank you, so I nod, too stunned to speak.

"You've been in and out of consciousness for the last few days."

"Days?"

"Yes, days, Gray. Do you realize how close you were to dying? You scared the shit out of me!"

"Sorry, I don't know what happened or how I got to your place. The last thing I remember was being in Dimitri's office. I'm sorry I scared you. I'm…I'm sorry for everything I've done recently."

"It's okay. I understand what you were doing by pushing me away."

"You do?"

"Marcus explained everything."

"Marcus was here?"

"You have him listed as your emergency contact. The hospital called him."

"Oh, I forgot that I had put him on there. Where is he now?"

"He left a few hours ago and said he had something to take care of."

"Something to take care of? Did he say where he was going?"

"No, he just took off once you were out of surgery, and they said you were out of the woods."

"Fuck, we have to go now!"

"What do you mean? What's going on?"

"Marcus probably went back to Midnight to confront Dimitri."

I try to lift myself up but can barely move without the pain taking my breath away.

"What are you talking about! You can't go anywhere in your condition."

"Hannah, please, I'm begging you. They'll kill Marcus if we don't do something. Help me out of this bed, now. Please!"

She's torn, and I can see it in her eyes. She wants to help Marcus but is also worried about me.

Fuck, I'm going to have to tell her the truth.

"Hannah, can I borrow your phone then?"

"My phone?"

"Yes, can I please borrow your phone? I need to make a call."

Reluctantly she passes her phone to me, and I dial the only number I have committed to memory.

"This is Agent Alexander. I need support to Club Midnight to assist an agent in apprehending Dimitri Ruez."

As I speak into the phone, I keep my eyes glued to Hannah and watch as she begins to realize that I'm not who I've said I was and that I'm entirely different.

"I've been working with your father and the D.A.'s office to apprehend Dimitri for several months. Marcus is my partner. We've both been undercover at Midnight's, hoping to catch Dimitri in some illegal activities. We have been helping your dad build his case."

She sits back, dropping my hand and moving away from me.

"When you first walked into Midnight, I had no idea who you were. It wasn't until after the first date or two that I realized who you were and how…complicated things could get. I had to find a way out that would keep you out of Midnight's for your safety."

I stop gasping for breath against the pain in my side and chest.

"You've been lying to me the whole time? Is your name even Gray?"

"Yes, Gray Alexander is my actual name. I swear I couldn't tell you I was working with your dad. I had to keep that to myself."

"And the other woman that James found you with?"

"Staged, she's another agent. It was the only way to keep you from getting involved and dragged further into this."

"You could have just told me the truth. I would have understood. I would have listened to what you were saying. I'm not a child, Gray. I understand complicated things. You should have just told me."

"I'm sorry, Hannah. I'm really sorry."

She's standing now with angry tears trailing down her face. I've betrayed her trust in every way possible.

"Please…Hannah." I'm reaching for her as she backs away. Her face told me all I needed to know. Turning, she leaves the room.

Shit.

I should have told her the truth, but her father and the department wouldn't have liked it that much.

Slowly sitting up, I pull the covers aside and swing my legs over the edge of the hospital bed.

I've got to get to Midnight to make sure that Marcus is alright, and that the agency responded in time.

For now, I'll put Hannah aside and deal with Marcus and Dimitri. Then I'll adequately explain myself and apologize to Hannah once we've wrapped everything up. I've got to believe she'll forgive me once she knows everything.

CHAPTER 62

Hannah

My mind is racing.

How could Gray lie to me about who she is and what she does? Did my father know about Gray, and did he lie to me as well?

Did everyone but me know?

Lying is one of the worst things someone can do. Suddenly, finding out that everyone I know has been lying to me has my head spinning. I'm hurt on so many levels I'm not sure if this is something I can ever forgive.

I don't know where Kee and James are as I leave the hospital. I need some fresh air and am too confused to care that I'm not supposed to be outside alone. They can all go to hell and enjoy each others' company there. I'm done with everyone and want to be alone.

"Ms. Winters?"

The voice comes from a car behind me that I didn't even notice had pulled up.

"Yes?"

I'm suddenly grabbed from behind by someone and shoved towards the car's back seat.

"What are you doing? Let me go! Help! Someone help!"

I look over my shoulder, shouting, and see two other body-guards, Ryan and Cole, rushing towards me as rough hands grab my arms and pull me towards the car.

I see Kee and James both run out of the hospital towards me. They're too far away, and I know none of the security will reach me in time.

"Hannah!" Kee shouts as James pulls his weapon. The men push me harder towards the car, placing me in front of them so James can't shoot.

I try to break away, but their grip on my arm is too firm as they dig their fingers into the flesh of my arm.

Ryan and Cole approach the front of the vehicle, guns are drawn, and Kee and James approach from the rear. I'm pushed into the car as James and Kee approach with guns drawn. Kee is on her radio as well. I look through the window at them as my assailants enter the car, drawing their weapons.

"Get them out of the way," the driver says coldly as he turns the key.

The man in the passenger seat draws his gun and, holding out the window, opens fire on the bodyguards approaching the front of the car.

"No! Stop!" I shout, seeing Cole go down as a bloom of red appears on the front of his white shirt.

Kee and James open fire from behind the vehicle as the driver presses the gas pedal, propelling the car forward.

Ryan has to throw himself out of the way to avoid being hit, and we narrowly miss running over Cole's prone body on the ground.

I close my eyes and try to steady myself as we gain speed. I look out the back window and see people rushing forward to help Cole, but I know it will be too late. The shot was fatal, and even with the best medical treatment, it's unlikely that Cole survived the wound.

Silent tears run down my face.

"Ms. Winters, we've been asked to bring you to see Mr. Ruez. He has some questions for you about your father."

"What are you saying? Where are you taking me?"

"Please, just sit back and relax. We'll be there in no time."

"You want me to fucking relax! You just kidnapped me off the street! I want to know where you're taking me right fucking now!"

They ignore me, and the ride continues in silence. The thought of jumping out of the moving vehicle crosses my mind as I turn to look at where we are. Before I can move, the man next to me takes a gun from his jacket.

"Don't do anything stupid, Ms. Winters."

Sighing, I sit back and resign myself to whatever fate has in store for me, all the time thinking about Gray. I can't help but worry for them when I should be worrying about myself.

CHAPTER 63

Gray

I can't breathe.

I'm on my hands and knees outside the hospital, watching Hannah be pulled away by one of Dimitri's men.

Every breath is a dagger in my left side as I struggle to stand, the hospital staff pulling me to my feet.

"I have to go. I have to get to Hannah."

"Agent Alexander, we can't let you go yet. You're not in any condition to leave the hospital!"

Pushing the nurses aside, I start walking in the direction the vehicle went when James grabs my arm.

"They took her. They took her," I manage to choke the words out around my pained breathing. Now that I've said it aloud, the reality of what's happened sinks in, and I feel my knees going out.

James catches me and helps me sit as Kee runs up.

"I got the license plates, and the police are running them," Kee says.

"Dimitri… They were Dimitri's men." I'm trying to catch my breath, but the pain in my side worsens. Every breath feels like fire in my lungs and glass across my skin.

"Where would they take her?"

"Probably the warehouse. It's the only place I can think they would take her."

"Okay, Kee and I will go there."

"I'm going, too."

"Gray, you can barely walk."

"I'm going, so let's stop talking about it and go."

They help me up, and we walk to their car.

"Wait!" Cassie runs out of the hospital with a syringe in hand. "If you insist on going, let me give you some pain meds. You can't move too much. It'll make your injuries worse, you understand?"

Nodding, I let Cassie inject the meds and immediately feel a warmth spreading through my body.

"Not too much," I mutter as she steps away.

"Bring her back safe, please. She's my best friend."

Nodding, I let Cassie help me into the sedan's back seat.

"What should we expect?" Kee asks, getting into the passenger seat.

"Dimitri usually has four guys with him, but he'll likely have more, given the situation. We can expect at least ten men, well-armed. They'll likely secure the bottom floor with Hannah on the second floor, with Dimitri and some of his men."

"Copy. Do you need to call it in?"

"Yeah, let me borrow a phone."

"Agent Alexander here. Have you heard from Marcus? No, we're heading to Dimitri's warehouse. If there isn't any activity at Midnight, redirect them to the warehouse, we expect resistance."

Hanging up, I hand the phone back to Kee and settle into the seat, trying to take a few moments to catch my breath and ease the pain in my burning side.

"We're pulling up now." James' voice wakes me. I must have dozed off on the ride over.

"Park a block away, and we'll walk in from there. Are you both armed?"

"Affirmative"

"We move together. Only fire if you have to, and don't fire if Hannah is in the area. You understand?"

"We've got it, Gray. Let's go."

James and Kee lead the way, and I follow closely behind them. Painfully aware that even if we make it past the first group on level one, I can do little to help them out.

James pushes the door open slowly, and we wait for gunfire to erupt. To our surprise, there's nothing but silence.

Did I make a mistake? Would they have taken her somewhere else?

We continue forward, crouching where we can for cover. Kee takes the right, James and I take the left. I follow closely behind him, one hand on his lower back to let him know where I am. We all move forward as one, eyes peeled.

"James, if we can, let's take them out without using a weapon. It'll be quieter and give us the element of surprise."

James nods, and we continue forward, approaching the first of Dimitri's men. James stalks forward, putting the man in a headlock and quickly and quietly laying him down as he loses consciousness.

One down.

Looking right, I see Kee struggling to subdue another one of Dimitri's men and move to help her, only to have the pain in my side bring me up short. James goes to assist instead, and they deftly handle the man.

I stay where I am. I feel completely useless, and Kee and James move forward as one unit.

It's probably best for me to lay low as they deal with Dimitri's men so I stay out of their way and don't cause more issues. I want nothing more than to run through the warehouse and find Hannah, but I know going slow and eliminating any threats is the best course of action.

James removes another obstacle, and Kee motions for me to move forward with them as we climb the stairs.

We've only taken care of three men. There has to be more.

A sudden noise from the second floor makes all of us stand up a little straighter. The hair on the back of my neck rises, and I move forward without even thinking.

Hannah.

Crying out in pain.

We all move towards the back staircase leading to the second floor.

I can hear other muffled voices from the second floor and only assume that it's Dimitri and some of his men.

We proceed up the stairs slowly. James is in the front, Kee is bringing in the rear, and I'm in the middle. Completely useless.

Fuck.

As we breach the second floor, we're surprised that the initial landing is empty, with no security, Dimitri, or Hannah.

The voices seem to be coming from the back room of the second floor. Moving forward, I can see James preparing himself to enter the room. His gun is drawn, his breath steady. He's ready.

I've no doubt that Kee is ready behind me. They know what they're doing. I'm the liability here. But none of that matters as long as we get Hannah, and she's okay. I don't care about anything else right now. Hannah is what's important. I'll do anything to get her back and ensure she's safe. I'll do all of the things that I should have done from the beginning.

James gives the signal, and we open the door at the back of the second floor.

CHAPTER 64

Hannah

Dimitri backhands me across the face, and I can't help but cry out in surprise and pain at the bite of the strike.

Oh my God, I'm so screwed. How am I going to get out of this one?

Dimitri stands in front of me, hands on his waist, waiting for me to answer his questions. The problem is that I have no idea what he's talking about. I know nothing about my father's cases. I'm not close to my father. He doesn't tell me anything but no matter how often I tell Dimitri that he doesn't believe me. He doesn't think that I don't know anything.

I look to the left at Marcus, unconscious on the floor. He's been out of it since they brought me here. I have no idea where he came from or what happened to him, but he's been unconscious for so long that I'm starting to worry about him. They have his hands bound behind his back, and I can see blood running down the side of his face.

My hands are tied to the arms of the chair along with my ankles. I can't move at all. The more I struggle, the tighter the ropes get, and the skin on my wrists is already worn raw and bleeding.

"Tell me what your father knows about my business." Dimitri snarls again.

"I told you, I don't know anything! My father doesn't tell me anything! I can't help you!" I prepare for another blow. Even though I know it's coming, it catches me by surprise, and my teeth click together as I gasp at the pain.

My ears are ringing, and I swear I can hear Gray's voice for a second, but that can't be possible. I must be concussed or something.

"Dimitri! You son of a bitch, don't touch her."

Gray! I turn quickly to see Gray at the door. Gray is pale and sweaty from pain and slightly bent over as she tries to relieve the pain of her broken ribs.

"Gray!" Gray's hurt because of me, here because of me, and I don't want to be responsible for them being hurt more. I struggle against the ropes, trying to get loose and free.

"Gray, run, get out of here!"

Gray doesn't fight back as Dimitri's men grab her arms and drag her forward. She can barely stay on her feet, let alone fight back.

What was she thinking about coming here?

"Marcus!" Gray cries out in surprise. "Marcus!"

Dimitri gives the signal, and one of his men lands a blow to Gray's stomach, causing her to fold over in pain. I can see Gray trying to catch her breath as she goes to her knees, holding her ribs.

"Stop, please, please just stop."

"I'll stop when you tell me what I want to know." Dimitri smirks.

"She doesn't know anything, Dimitri. She and her father aren't close. They don't talk. She really doesn't know anything. I know more about the case than she does. If you want to talk to someone, talk to me," Gray manages each word with a gasp, and her voice is full of pain.

"Gray, don't." I try my wrists again, only to feel the skin tearing under the ropes. Biting my bottom lip until I taste blood, I work the ropes more. I know I can get out of them. I need to work the knots a little more. As the cord becomes slick with my blood, the knot gives. Not a lot but enough to give me hope. I keep working at it, feeling the rope bite into my fingertips and wrists.

"Get her up and bring her over here. Between the two of them, we might get some answers."

Dimitri's men reach down to grab Gray again, only this time, Gray is ready for them. I see it in her eyes and know there will be a fight. I brace myself.

From behind the door, James and Kee suddenly appear, guns drawn and aimed at the remaining men around Dimitri and Gray. Gray stands up quickly, catching them off guard, and lands a well-placed blow on one of the men. Before he can recover, she drives her knee into his face, leveling him.

"Give up, Dimitri. There are more men outside. You'll never make it out of here," Gray pants, but it's clear she means business.

Dimitri seems to panic for a moment before pulling his gun. I feel the cold steel against my temple.

"I think I'm the one with the upper hand here, Gray. Why don't you all put your weapons down."

It's now or never. The rope quietly falls to the ground as I free my hands. Without hesitation, I throw myself backward in my chair while reaching up to grab Dimitri's hand.

CHAPTER 65

Gray

Shit.

I wasn't expecting Dimitri to be armed with a gun. A knife, yes, but not a gun. He hates guns and rarely carries them.

I glance at James and Kee, looking for support, an idea, or anything to get Dimitri to focus on us, not Hannah.

Out of the corner of my eye, I see Marcus stir. This might be our distraction if Marcus is aware enough to pull it off.

I move towards Dimitri with my hands up. "Take it easy, Dimitri. Let's just take it easy. Why don't you let Hannah go, and I'll go with you. As I said, I know more about the case than she does. I'll tell you everything."

"Now you want to chat. Why don't you come over here? I think I'll take both of you with me instead. Slowly."

"Right. Nice and slow." I start walking towards him. Keeping my eyes fixed on Hannah, trying to lend her strength and courage as Dimitri shoves the gun harder into her temple.

"Easy, Dimitri," I say again as I move closer to him and Hannah. I can see Marcus getting to his knees. I need to distract Dimitri to make this work.

I take another step, moving closer to him. I'm about three steps away when I decide to make my move, hoping that Marcus is on his feet and able to move.

But before we can move, Hannah throws herself backward, driving the chair she's in against Dimitri's legs while reaching up to grab the gun.

Without hesitating, I lunge towards Dimitri, and at the same time, Marcus lunges for Hannah, who is still falling backward as Dimitri stumbles back.

Several things happen at once.

James and Kee fire their guns, a third gun goes off, Hannah cries out, and I feel a stinging pain in my shoulder before slamming into Dimitri.

I don't have the strength to get up as Dimitri takes off, but before he can make it a few steps, Hannah scrambles to her knees, grabs the chair she was tied to, and throws it towards Dimitri. It's a perfectly aimed throw, and Dimitri's legs get tangled with the chair, causing him to tumble to the dusty cold warehouse floor. James is on him in an instant. Zip ties his hands behind his back as the room is suddenly full of people in black.

Back up finally arrives. I scoff softly and glance at Marcus on his side, gathering himself. Kee is helping Hannah up and checking on Marcus.

Hannah's hands are covered in blood. She did so well. She stayed calm and took control of the situation.

Pride swells in my chest before being chased away from the pain that's suddenly all-consuming. Burning through my chest and shoulder.

I need to rest for a moment and catch my breath.

"Gray!"

The next thing I know, I'm in an ambulance, and Hannah frantically calls my name.

"I'm okay." Or at least that's what I try to say, but I can't seem to get my mouth or throat to work right. I must make some noise because Hannah floats into my view.

"You're okay. I'm here, you're okay, you're okay." She keeps repeating it over and over again.

I try again, "What happened?" The words come out muffled from behind the oxygen mask but must make some sense.

"You were shot! He shot you in the shoulder, you're going to be fine, but you've lost a lot of blood."

"Marcus?"

"Marcus is banged up pretty good and is in the other ambulance with Kee." Hannah gives me a little smile that I can't help but return, even though everything hurts. "I think she has a thing for him."

I nod my agreement and close my eyes. I'm exhausted and want nothing more than to sleep.

"I could go for some Chinese?" I manage as sleep tugs at my consciousness.

"Only if it's in the sunroom." She leans forward, takes the oxygen mask away, and kisses me.

"Deal." I nod again and let the sleep take me under.

CHAPTER 66

Hannah

"Gray's in surgery for the bullet wound and for her lung. Marcus took a pretty bad hit to the head but should be fine." Cassie informs Kee and me.

"Thanks, Cassie." I can't help but give Kee a huge grin and hug. "Any idea of when we'll be able to see them?"

"You can check in on Marcus, but it'll be long before you see Gray. I'll keep you in the loop."

"Thanks, Cas."

Kee, James, and I head towards Marcus' room. Kee takes the lead and walks up to Marcus' bed, asking him how he feels.

I feel a slight smile tugging on the corners of my mouth as Kee stands next to Marcus' bed, even taking his hand in hers!

I look sideways to James, who seems as shocked as I feel.

"James, I think we should leave," I whisper, backing slowly out of the room to give them space.

James nods and follows closely behind me as we retreat back to the waiting room.

"When did that happen?" he asks.

"James! It's been happening the whole time! How did you not notice?"

"Are you serious? I ignore that kind of stuff. It's just weird."

"James! I can't believe you! Kee's your partner. How can you not notice that she's head over heels for that guy!?"

James shrugs and walks off, leaving me giggling at how oblivious he is. Now that he's gone, it's just me in the waiting room, worrying about Gray. I know they're in excellent hands, but I can't help but worry about them. I'm anxious to check in and see how they're doing. I want to know that Gray is okay. I can look past everything that has happened and the lies. I just want them. No, I need them to be alright.

"Doctor Winters? You can see Gray now. She's awake."

CHAPTER 67

Gray

've been awake for about an hour now. Piecing together what happened. My arm and chest hurt like a son of a bitch but other than that, I think I'm in okay shape. The nurse was kind enough to tell me that Marcus was in recovery and that Hannah's wrists and hands would be fine.

Hannah walks in, silencing the worry and questions floating through my brain.

"Hannah." It comes out a whisper, almost a plea, as I reach for her with my right hand. She comes forward immediately, wiping tears as she walks to me.

She takes my hand in her bandaged fingers and gently folds me into a hug, making sure not to hit my shoulder or broken ribs.

"You're alright," she whispers. I nod, not trusting myself to be able to speak right now as the emotions close my throat. "Everyone's okay," she says, staying in my hold a little longer before pulling away to look at me.

It's my first time getting a good look at her since Dimitri took her captive, and seeing the bruises on her face makes my heart rate jump with anger. I reach up, caressing the bruises softly and taking in the state of her.

I look down at her bandaged hands and, picking up the right one, gently kiss the tips of each finger before kissing the inside of her bandaged wrist.

Her sniffles become soft giggles as I continue my kisses on her left hand.

"How long will you be out of work with these?" I asked, holding her hands in mine.

"I'm not sure, but at least my dad will finally get his wish of me taking leave."

I smile at her and pull her forward for a kiss, smiling as my heart rate spikes on the monitor.

She pulls away, smiling as well and looking at the monitor. "We should take it easy until you're fully recovered."

I roll my eyes pulling her in for another kiss. "I don't know if that's a deal."

Keep reading for a look at Book 2 of the Fall Trilogy

Fall Into Me: Kee and Marcus

2 Months after *Fall into Midnight*

CHAPTER 1

Marcus

The bullet was close enough that I heard the air push away from it as it whizzed just over my head.

Returning fire, I use the distraction to run to the stack of box crates to my right and duck behind them as Kiera's men return fire.

I've been tracking her for the last month since she went on the lamb, taking Dimitri's business dealings with her. I finally found her, but getting close enough to her to get revenge is the problem.

Kiera and her father have caused so much damage to Gray and Hannah's lives, not to mention the people they impact through their drug running. Someone has to stop them.

A bullet hits the wood beside my face sending splinters fanning through the air. A few find their way into my skin as I recoil too slowly to avoid them. I've gotten too close this time to give up, but I'm outnumbered and outgunned. Not to mention I'm almost out of ammo.

Shit. I'm going to have to make a run for it.

Every fiber of my body tells me to run, but my stubbornness makes me stay put. Perhaps I'll be able to make a move. Just a little longer. Maybe they'll slip up.

Looking around the side of the crates, I can see another set of them a bit further up. I'll have a better angle if I can make it to that bunch. My gut clenches as I prepare to make a dash for the farther crates. I steady myself, feeling my heart beating wildly in my chest and my cramping muscles. If I'm going to make it, I need to calm myself and have a clear head. I take another deep calming breath.

A lull in the gunfire means they're either waiting for my next move or reloading. Hopefully, it's the latter. I burst forward from my protected position and make for the other stack.

Pain blossoms in my upper thigh.

Fuck. I've been hit!

I feel myself pitching forward and to the side as my leg gives out, sending me sprawling to the dirty concrete floor of the warehouse. My weapon flies from my hands as I try to brace for impact.

Rookie move.

I hit hard, feeling the impact on my wrists and knees as I catch myself enough to keep moving forward. I crawl towards the crates and what meager shelter they offer. Without my gun, I'm pretty much screwed. I know it, and so do they.

How will I get out of this one?

I can hear them speaking in Russian as they start to surround me. Pulling out my phone, I text the location of the warehouse to the only number in it.

I hope she understands why I did this. I should have told her how I felt. Shit, too late now.

I remove my belt and make a tourniquet above the gunshot wound, hoping to slow the bleeding. I get to my feet, feeling the world tilt as the blood loss hits me. I'm not going down without a fight.

I won't let Kiera win that easily.

CHAPTER 2

Kee

I t's been a month since Marcus fell off the grid. No matter how hard I look for him, I can't figure out where he disappeared.

Gray said he took the month to recover from his injuries and take some time off from work.

I'm hurt in a way that leaves me more angry than sad. I know they're hiding something from me. I thought Marcus and I had something going. I felt that he trusted me, especially after everything with Dimitri.

We'd spent several weeks together as he recovered from his injuries. He even stayed here at Hannah's with Gray and the rest of us as he recovered. I thought we had grown close enough that he wouldn't just up and leave without a word.

Gray gets weekly updates from him, but she doesn't share them with me. I'm not sure what that's about, but it annoys the hell out of me.

Is he avoiding me on purpose? What has he been up to for the last month, and when will he return?

"Penny, for your thoughts?" James' voice snaps me out of it.

"Mind your own business, James," I growl, getting up from the table and heading out the front door to take up my post across the street from Hannah's. I know I'm harsh with James, but I can't help my frustration.

Climbing into the car, I slam the door and turn on the radio. It's cold here, and the dreary weather does nothing to lift my even darker spirits.

We're still providing security for Hannah as the case against Dimitri is still being built. As the D.A.'s daughter, she's in almost as much danger as her father is. We've got a little extra help now that Gray lives here. Although she's still recovering from her wounds from our encounter with Dimitri over a month ago. It is nice to have another set of eyes. It gives James and me a bit of a break occasionally.

Fucking Marcus.

I'm all kinds of distracted right now, and it's because of him. I feel disgusted for letting someone throw me off my game like he has. There's just something about him that puts me at ease, and I miss his goofy ass.

I can't stop thinking about his 6'3" frame, salt, and peppered hair. Not to mention how the skin around his eyes crinkles when he smiles and laughs and how he's so caring and gentle while looking like he could kill you with a single blow.

Ugh, Kee, snap out of it!

I'm so gone for this guy. I should have never let this happen. I hate myself for it! I blame it on Gray and Hannah for showing me that you can love and be loved while still being strong and independent. It's definitely all their fault.

Watching them fall for each other and become closer, even when everything was working against them, was beautiful. Although all of the PDA was a bit much, it was still pretty adorable.

I can't help but smile as I look at the front of Hannah's house, knowing that Hannah and Gray are cuddled up in the sunroom right now, all cute and shit.

I need to get Gray to tell me what she knows about Marcus.

The smile slips from my face.

CHAPTER 3

Marcus

I come to as a scream rips through my raw and shattered throat. Everything hits me all at once. I'm hanging from my hands, wrapped and bound by chains draped over a solid wooden beam. My clothes are gone except for my shorts. My thigh is on fire, along with the other wounds scattered across my body. The worst is a large gash running from my belly button to my side. It's deep, and blood is still streaming, forming a pool at my bare feet that barely scrape the concrete floor.

I'm no longer in the warehouse, although this looks to be a similar location. It's hard to breathe, and I can't feel my hands anymore, so I've been hanging here for a while. I try to grip the chain above my hands to pull myself up to relieve pressure from my chest and shoulders, but I can't get my hands to work right.

As I dangle there, flashes from my last moments of consciousness come flooding back. I'd tried to surprise Kiera's men by leaping from behind the crates before they could reach me. It worked but only briefly. It wasn't long before they had converged on me, kicking the living shit out of me, until I lost consciousness. I remember hearing Kiera's voice telling them not to kill me and that she wanted me alive.

It would have been better to have died then than to be hanging in a warehouse completely bared for Kiera's twisted mind to play with. I feel helpless, and panic builds in my chest as I look around at the space I'm in.

In front of me, there's a table with a chair…and *tools*. Various things that cut, ply, stick, stab, and more, including a cart close by that has what looks like a car battery on it. I've seen these kinds of instruments before. They're used for interrogations as instruments of torture. I can only imagine how thrilled Kiera will be as she electrocutes my ass.

I hope my last text went through. It's my only hope that anyone will know what happened to me. I hope Gray will understand what it means and know I'm in some deep shit. I've got to prepare myself for what's to come. There's no telling how long it will take for someone to notice I'm missing and to come looking. Especially if the text didn't go through.

A door opened behind me, and Kiera's wicked chuckling sent a shiver down my spine despite steeling myself.

"You're finally awake! For a moment, I thought maybe we'd been too hard on you!" Kiera walks into view with a Cheshire cat smile, stretching her face abnormally from ear to ear. If every person is the embodiment of evil, it's Kiera. She has no moral compass.

"Good to see you too, Kiera. You're looking well." That's what she knows me as. My plan is to keep it as light and silly as I can. The goofy old guy from the club, I can play that up and hopefully use it to my advantage. The less she thinks I'm a threat, the lower her guard.

Make them think you're weaker than you are, Marcus. Rule number one of being tortured.

"You're so polite, Marcus! I wouldn't expect anything less from you. Did you know that you used to be one of my father's favorites? He absolutely loved your manners. That stupid old man let his feelings blind him."

She moves to the table, dragging the single chair out from under it and turning it to face me. Sitting, she crosses her legs and stares at me with hunger, interest, and disgust.

I stare back, keeping my face blank and as passive as possible.

I'm not a threat.

I need her to believe it. It's my only chance of surviving this.

A slow smile turns her blood-red lips up, forming more of a snarl as she runs her tongue across her top teeth. Reaching out, she runs a finger over the solid steel instruments on the table.

"Now, where shall we begin?"

Thank you for reading *Fall into Midnight*,
Book 1 of the Fall Series.
If you enjoyed this book, please help spread
the word by leaving an online review.

KEEP IN TOUCH WITH ARDEN COUTTS

WEBSITE: ardencoutts.com
INSTAGRAM: @ardencoutts